PUPPY PATROL ™

PUPPY SCHOOL

JENNY DALE

Illustrations by Mick Reid

Cover illustration by Michael Rowe

AN
APPLE
PAPERBACK

SCHOLASTIC INC.
New York Toronto London Auckland Sydney
Mexico City New Delhi Hong Kong Buenos Aires

SPECIAL THANKS TO NARINDER DHAMI

No part of this publication may be reproduced in whole or in part, or stored in a
retrieval system, or transmitted in any form, or by any means, electronic,
mechanical, photocopying, recording, or otherwise, without written permission
of the publisher. For information regarding permission,
write to Macmillan Publishers Ltd., 25 Eccleston Place,
London SW1W 9NF and Basingstoke.

ISBN 0-439-21815-2

All rights reserved. Published by Scholastic Inc., 555 Broadway, New York, NY
10012 by arrangement with Macmillan Children's Books,
a division of Macmillan Publishers Ltd.

SCHOLASTIC and associated logos are trademarks and/or registered trademarks
of Scholastic Inc.

12 11 10 9 8 7 6 5 4 3 2 1   1 2 3 4 5 6/0

Printed in the U.S.A.   40
First Scholastic printing, September 2001

CHAPTER ONE

"**B**rr, it's freezing!" Neil Parker complained as he and his younger sister, Emily, walked briskly across the field, their breath steaming in the frosty morning air. "Did you notice how cold it was in school yesterday? I bet Mr. Grundy's turned the heat down again!"

"He's so mean!" Emily said indignantly. Then she began to laugh. "And so grumpy! Julie and I call him Grumpy Grundy!"

Neil grinned. "Good one, Em. He's been at Meadowbank for a couple of months now, and I haven't seen him smile once, yet."

"Maybe he's not a principal at all," Emily said, shaking her dark brown hair out of her eyes. "Maybe he's really an alien who's come to conquer Earth and take over our minds."

"Well, he won't have much trouble with yours!" Neil teased her. Then he turned around to check where Sam, his black-and-white Border collie, had gone to. It was Saturday morning and they were taking Sam for a quick walk up the hill before breakfast. It was one of Neil's favorite dog-walking routes near their home in Compton.

Sam had stopped to sniff at something interesting on the road.

"Here, boy!" Neil called. Sam immediately bounded toward him, wagging his feathery plume of a tail. He was a handsome dog, with a thick, shaggy coat and dark eyes that were always alert and eager. Neil bent down and patted him, thinking, as he always did, how impossible it was that Sam could really be sick when he looked so bright and lively.

"Good boy!"

Neil had to keep a sharp eye on Sam. The collie had recently been diagnosed with a heart murmur after collapsing at the end of an important Agility competition. Sam had won the contest, but that was hardly any consolation for Neil. One day, Sam's heart would simply give out, and Neil hated to think about it. For now, though, Sam was a healthy, happy dog and the apple of Neil Parker's eye.

"I don't see why Mr. Grundy has to be so miserable," Emily persisted as they walked up the road with Sam. "You would think he didn't like children."

"He probably doesn't," Neil replied. "And I bet he doesn't like dogs, either." To Neil, anyone who didn't like dogs was definitely a little odd.

Dogs were the most important things in the world to Neil. He sometimes wondered if that was because he lived at King Street Kennels or if he had just been born loving dogs. Neil liked to think that maybe it was a little of both.

King Street Kennels was run by Neil and Emily's parents, Bob and Carole Parker. They took in boarders, but they also cared for abandoned dogs in their rescue center. Neil was surrounded by dogs, day and night, and that was just the way he liked it.

Emily bent down to pat Sam's head. "Mr. Grundy certainly doesn't like guinea pigs, anyway. When he came into our classroom last week, he made me put Mortimer's cage outside in the hall."

Neil couldn't help smiling at his sister's tone of voice. "I think he should be in the army," he said, thinking about the new principal's tall, straight-backed figure and thick mustache. "I keep expecting him to shout 'Quick march!' when we go into assembly!"

"He's got a loud voice, too," Emily added as they reached the hill. "You can hear him shouting right across the playground."

"Maybe he'll settle down soon. You know how dogs sometimes take a while to settle in when they first arrive at the kennel."

Emily raised her eyebrows. "What kind of dog would Mr. Grundy be then?"

"A Rottweiler?" Neil suggested, with a grin.

Emily giggled. Then she pointed along the road. "Look, isn't that Mr. Hamley and Dotty?"

Neil squinted to see. A man with a dalmatian on a leash was walking along some distance ahead of them.

"Yes, it is. Come on, let's say hello. I haven't seen Dotty for a long time."

Mr. Hamley was Neil's teacher at Meadowbank

School, and his dalmatian, Dotty, was one of the most appealing, but also one of the naughtiest dogs that Neil had ever known. She had been such a boisterous bundle of chaos that the Hamleys had considered giving her away. Neil was determined to train her to follow instructions, and his efforts, along with his father's obedience classes, had eventually paid off.

Neil, Emily, and Sam hurried toward the crazy dalmatian. As soon as Dotty could smell them, she started pulling at her leash and barking loudly. Neil chuckled. Although she was much better behaved now, Dotty's training hadn't worked miracles! But she was a beautiful dog, well-proportioned and slender, with long, elegant legs and a sleek white coat covered in glossy black spots.

"Hello, Mr. Hamley," Neil called as they approached. He could see Dotty more closely now and his eyes widened in amazement. It wasn't always easy to tell when a dog was expecting puppies, but Neil could see that Dotty was. He nudged his sister as they walked up to Mr. Hamley and the dalmatian. "I think Dotty's going to be a mom!"

Emily hadn't noticed, but now she looked thrilled. "That's great!"

Neil knew what the signs were. He had helped out at the birth of Jake, Sam's son. Jake was still with his mother, Delilah, but as soon as he was old enough he'd be coming to live at King Street — a new puppy for Neil and the Parkers. Neil had never looked forward to anything more in his life.

"Hello, Neil, Emily." Paul Hamley smiled, then almost fell flat on his face as Dotty lunged toward them, taking her owner with her. "Down, Dotty!" he said firmly. Dotty dropped to the ground reluctantly, every muscle tensed, her liquid brown eyes staring up at Neil and Emily. Emily knelt down and put her arms around the dog's neck, and Dotty wagged her tail happily, trying to lick Emily's nose.

"Is Dotty having pups, Mr. Hamley?" Neil just managed to stop himself from sounding surprised. He knew how much of a handful Dotty could be, and he couldn't help wondering how the Hamleys, who also had a new baby, would cope.

"Yes, she is," Mr. Hamley said, beaming proudly at the excited dalmatian. The teacher was nicknamed Smiler because his teaching could hardly be described as fun-filled. When he was with Dottie, though, he was a lot more approachable. "They're due in about two weeks, around the fifteenth. She looks good, doesn't she?"

"Terrific," Neil agreed, kneeling down beside Emily to stroke the dog's beautifully marked coat. Delighted, Dotty stuck out her tongue and licked Neil's hand. "I didn't know you were going to breed Dotty, Mr. Hamley."

"Well, we weren't planning to," Mr. Hamley replied,

"but a friend of mine has a dalmatian named Ainsley, and he persuaded us to . . ."

"Mate the dogs?" Neil asked.

"Yes." Mr. Hamley said.

"Are you going to keep the puppies, Mr. Hamley?" Emily asked curiously. The Hamleys could barely cope with Dotty as it was, let alone a bunch of lively little puppies.

Mr. Hamley looked alarmed. "No, no, but we'll find them good homes, of course. To be honest, we thought it might calm Dottie down if she became a mom."

Neil and Emily looked at Dottie, who was now jumping around Mr. Hamley's legs playing hide-and-seek with Sam, and then at each other. They both knew what the other was thinking. Fat chance!

"You must be very busy with your baby," Emily said politely as a rather flustered Mr. Hamley ordered Dotty to sit.

He nodded. "Yes, and the beginning of the year at school is always the busiest time, too. And now, with a new principal as well . . ." Mr. Hamley's voice trailed away.

Neil suddenly noticed how tired he was looking and realized that it must be hard for everyone, including the teachers, to adapt to a new principal, especially a principal like Mr. Grundy.

"Well, I must be going home." Mr. Hamley seemed to pull himself up sharply, as if he'd realized that he shouldn't be complaining about his workload to two students. "I'll see you on Monday. Come along, Dotty."

"Just a minute, Mr. Hamley," Neil said quickly. He'd suddenly thought of a good way to help out the teacher and Dotty.

"Yes?" Mr. Hamley turned back, looking grumpy himself.

"I could walk Dotty for you sometimes," Neil suggested. "Would that help?"

Mr. Hamley seemed taken aback for a moment. "That's a very generous offer, Neil. Are you sure you wouldn't mind?" Then he laughed as he looked at Neil's eager face. "No, of course you wouldn't!"

Neil arranged to come for Dotty on Monday after

school. Then he and Emily said their good-byes and headed back to King Street Kennels.

"I wish Mr. Hamley was our principal instead of Mr. Grundy," Emily sighed. "I wonder why he didn't get the job? Mrs. Hamley told Mom he'd applied for it."

Neil shrugged. "Obviously Grumpy Grundy had something that Smiler didn't."

"Like what?"

"Mom said she thinks the school board wanted someone who could save the school some money. Haven't you noticed how Mr. Grundy's been going around to all the classrooms, counting everything and checking how many books we have? We never get new pencils or erasers anymore."

"I'm down to my last well-chewed stub!" Emily remarked as they arrived home.

The Parkers lived in the countryside on the outskirts of town. The kennel buildings were at the back of the house, built around a square courtyard. It was just as well they had no close neighbors because there was a constant sound of dogs barking. There were other buildings, too: Red's Barn, where Bob Parker held his twice-weekly obedience classes, and also the small block of kennels that housed the rescue center.

Even though it was still early, King Street was already open for business. Neil and Emily headed for the kennel office, and Sam trotted off to have a drink and then a snooze under his favorite hedge in the backyard. Kate McGuire, the kennel assistant, was in the office, looking pale and very sad and blowing her nose into a tissue.

"Hello, Kate," Neil said with a frown. "What's wrong?"

Kate attempted a smile. "Your dad told me to go home," she said in a hoarse voice. "I think I'm getting that flu that's been going around."

Neil and Emily looked sympathetic. They all liked Kate. She was great with the dogs and was almost like one of the family.

"I'm going to take Kate home in a minute or two." Bob Parker, a large, well-built man with thick, dark hair and a shaggy beard, came up behind them. "Your mother's feeding the dogs by herself in Block One, so if you two want to give her a hand . . ."

"Sure," Neil said, delighted. "Where's Squirt?"

As if on cue, his little sister Sarah appeared.

"Can I come with you to take Kate home, Dad?" she asked.

Bob shook his head. "We don't want you coming down with the flu, too, sweetheart."

"Poor Kate," Sarah said, patting the kennel assistant's arm. "I'll paint you a picture of all the dogs in the kennel. That'll make you feel better."

Neil and Emily grinned at each other. Sarah's response to any crisis, big or small, was to paint a picture — usually of a dog.

"Come on, Squirt," Neil said. "You can help us with the morning feeding."

Neil, Sarah, and Emily crossed the courtyard and stepped into Kennel Block One. Both kennel blocks were light and spacious with ten pens on each side of a central aisle. Their mother was unlocking the pen of a large black mongrel. She held a bowl of dog biscuits in her hand. Duke had been left there a couple of days ago by his owners, Mr. and Mrs. Carter, who had gone on vacation. The dog was slumped in a corner, looking miserable, but as Carole walked into the pen, he slowly stood up.

"Guess what, Mom?" Neil called. "Dotty's having pups!"

"Really?" Carole Parker raised her eyebrows. She was a tall, striking-looking woman with short black hair and a brisk, no-nonsense manner. "Well, let's hope it calms her down a bit, although I wouldn't bet on it!"

"That's what we thought," Emily laughed.

"More puppies!" Sarah said, delighted. She had been thrilled when Sam and Delilah's puppies had been born, although she hadn't been at the birth. "I hope Dotty has lots and lots!"

"I don't," Neil said quickly. "I don't think Mr. Hamley could cope!"

"Maybe he and Dotty will surprise us all!" their mother said with a grin. She was inside Duke's pen now and the dog was on his feet, muscles tensed. He looked nervous. "Easy, boy," Carole said soothingly. "I've just come to give you some food. Nobody's going to hurt you."

For some reason the dog began growling a low, menacing sound deep in the back of his throat.

Neil began to feel alarmed. "What's the matter with him?" he muttered to Emily. "He was OK when I fed him yesterday." The dog hadn't been particularly friendly the previous evening, but Neil hadn't been surprised. Some dogs took longer to settle in at the kennel than others.

Carole Parker put the dish down, still talking to the dog in a reassuring voice. Suddenly Duke leaped forward, his jaws drawn back in a vicious snarl. As Neil, Emily, and Sarah watched, wide-eyed with horror, the dog pounced on their mother and sank his teeth into her hand.

Carole Parker screamed.

CHAPTER TWO

In a low voice, Neil warned Emily and Sarah to stay absolutely still and quiet as their mother stood up and hesitantly stepped out of the pen, her face pale and drawn. Almost as soon as he had bitten her, Duke had slunk off with his tail between his legs. He now sat hunched in the corner of his pen, staring at the floor.

Neil ran over to his mother, his heart thumping with anxiety. He pulled off his sweatshirt and held it out to her. She immediately wrapped it tightly around her right hand, trying to stop the flow of blood.

"Dad!" Emily yelled frantically, racing out of the kennel block toward the house. Sarah began to cry.

"What's the matter?" A moment later Bob ap-

peared in the open doorway with Kate close behind
him. "Carole, are you all right? What happened?"

"I went in to feed Duke . . ." Carole was obviously
in a great deal of pain and had to force the words
out, ". . . and he — he attacked me."

"He just seemed to go mad," Neil muttered. He
stared at the dog, which had retreated into his basket, looking as if he knew that he had done wrong.

"Did he break the skin?" Bob asked, gently trying
to take his wife's hand. "Is there any blood?"

Carole nodded and winced, biting down hard on
her lip as Bob unwrapped the sweatshirt. Horrified,
Neil caught a brief glimpse of blood pouring from a

large wound in his mother's hand. It looked even worse close-up. Bob, seeing the look on Neil's face, quickly wrapped the sweatshirt back into place.

"I'd better get you to the emergency room," he said. "You're going to need stitches."

"Mommy!" Sarah wailed, sobbing even harder.

"I'm fine, sweetheart," Carole said, making an effort to sound calm, but Neil had never seen her look so white and shocked before. "The hospital will fix me up soon."

"I'll stay with the kids while you two go to the ER," Kate said, putting her arm around Sarah.

"But you're not feeling well —" Carole began.

"Just go," Kate said firmly, fishing in the pocket of her jeans for a clean tissue to wipe Sarah's face. "We'll be fine."

"Thanks, Kate." Bob put his arm around his wife and led her away. "And none of you are to go into that dog's pen under *any* circumstances," he added sternly over his shoulder.

Neil felt sick as he watched his mother and father hurry off. It was distressing on the rare occasions when a dog suddenly turned vicious — especially when there didn't seem to be a good reason.

"Come on, Neil," Kate called out as she led Emily and Sarah toward the house. "Let's go inside and have a snack. Then we'll feed the rest of the dogs."

Neil looked around the kennel block before he followed the others. Most of the pens were occupied, but all the dogs were strangely subdued, as if they could sense that something was wrong. Duke was slumped in his basket, head between his paws, looking very sorry for himself.

"Why did you do it, boy?" Neil asked softly, wondering what was going to happen next. He knew that the police could take the owners of a dangerous dog to court and that could sometimes mean the dog being put down. It would probably all depend on whether or not Duke had ever done anything like this before.

It was around lunchtime when Neil heard the sound of the family Range Rover pulling into the driveway outside the house. He ran outside anxiously, followed by the others.

"Don't worry," Bob said cheerfully as he helped Carole out of the car. "Your mom has been well taken care of at the hospital, and she's fine."

Carole's hand was heavily bandaged and in a sling, but Neil was relieved to see that she looked better and had regained some color in her face.

"Of course I'm fine!" she said, putting her other arm around Sarah. "Now why don't you come inside and we'll have some lunch while your dad drives Kate home?"

"Oh, I can walk," Kate said heroically, sneezing into a tissue. "Bob must want his lunch."

"Lunch can wait. You look terrible, Kate," Bob told her.

"Thanks," Kate replied, grimacing.

"Can I come, Dad?" Neil asked. He wanted to have a private chat with his father about Duke.

Bob nodded, and the three of them climbed into the Range Rover. Neil told Kate and Bob that Dotty was expecting pups, but he didn't mention Duke until they'd dropped Kate off and were heading back home. Then he took a deep breath and turned to his dad.

"Dad, what's going to happen to Duke?"

His father looked grim. "I don't know, Neil. There's not a lot we can do about it until his owners come back, anyway."

"I don't understand why he suddenly turned on Mom like that."

Bob shrugged. "There are different reasons why dogs become aggressive. Duke might have been abused when he was a puppy, or it may be something to do with the way his present owners treat him."

"Will he have to be put down?" Neil persisted.

"It's hard to say." Bob swung the Range Rover expertly down the narrow country lane. "We'd have to take the owners to court if we think the dog should be put down, and let a judge decide."

Neil paused. He hated the thought of a young, healthy dog being put down, but seeing Duke attack his mom had terrified him. Duke was dangerous and unpredictable.

"Do you think he's bitten anyone before?"

"It's possible. But if he has, it was horribly irresponsible of the Carters not to let us know."

His father sounded really angry. They relied on the owners to give them as much information as they possibly could about their dogs. If they were less than truthful, this could be the result.

"Anyway," Bob went on, "I want to stop off at the police station and report this to Sergeant Moorhead. That makes it official."

Neil nodded. Sergeant Moorhead had been involved in a previous case involving a dangerous dog at King Street Kennels. Skye, a rough collie, had been wrongly accused of killing sheep, and Neil and Emily had found the real culprit. This time, though, Neil thought, there was no doubt who the guilty party was. . . .

"You were right to come and report it," Sergeant Moorhead remarked as he finished taking down Bob's and Neil's statements. Neil had been interviewed because he had seen the attack take place, and the policeman also wanted to speak to Carole herself. "What do you want to do now?"

Bob frowned. "We'll have to wait until the Carters come back from vacation, of course."

Sergeant Moorhead nodded. He was middle-aged, with short gray hair and a calm, controlled manner.

"Yes, but are you prepared to keep the dog at the kennel, or do you want me to take possession of him?"

"You mean you'll take him into custody, like you did with Skye?" Bob asked.

"We don't have any room in the police kennel at the moment," Sergeant Moorhead replied, "but I expect the SPCA would take him in."

"There's no point in moving the dog around." Bob made up his mind quickly. "We'll keep him until his owners come back, as long as my wife's happy with that."

Neil felt a pang of unhappiness as he and his father left the police station. It was extremely rare for any dog to stay at King Street Kennels under such a dark cloud. Neil couldn't help feeling depressed on Duke's behalf. The Carters were certainly in for a shock when they got back from their vacation.

"Dotty's *pregnant*?" Chris Wilson said incredulously as he and Neil bicycled through the school gates on Monday morning. "Old Smiler's going to have his hands full, isn't he?"

Neil nodded. "Especially if Dotty's pups take after their mother!" he pointed out.

Chris laughed. He was Neil's best friend, and they looked very much alike. They even had the same dark-brown spiky hair.

"I noticed Smiler was looking even more fed up

than usual, but I thought that was probably because of Mr. Grundy!"

"I wonder what surprises Grumpy has lined up for us today?" Neil remarked as they went over to the bike stands.

"Grumpy Grundy? Hey, I like it!" Chris said with a grin.

"It's what Emily calls him," Neil replied. "I think the name really suits him!"

"By the way, how's your mom?"

"She's all right," Neil replied. Carole Parker had

spent most of the weekend resting, but that morning she'd been up to get them off to school and she looked almost back to her usual self. "She can't use her hand that much though, and Kate has the flu. I hope she's back soon."

His mother hadn't objected to Duke staying at King Street, but Neil noticed that she hadn't been out into the kennels all weekend, and Bob, with help from Neil and Emily, had done all the feeding and walking of the dogs. It was tough on his father, Neil thought, because he and Emily couldn't help out that much when they were in school all day. But Bob hadn't thought much of Emily's suggestion that they should both take the week off from school to help out at home.

Chris glanced across the playground and nudged Neil in the ribs. "Here comes Grumpy," he whispered.

Mr. Grundy was striding across the playground, tall and stern, briefcase under arm, glaring at any child who happened to get in his way.

"Do you think he *ever* smiles?" Chris whispered.

Neil shook his head. "I don't think he'd smile even if he won the lottery!"

"Who won the lottery?" said a voice close to Neil's ear. "The Puppy Patrol?"

Neil looked around and saw Hasheem Lindon who was in his class. Hasheem was always teasing Neil about his obsession with dogs. The Parker family was now known throughout Compton as the Puppy Patrol — thanks to Hasheem.

"No such luck!" Neil grinned. "We were just talking about Mr. Grundy."

Hasheem rolled his eyes. "He's not a human being, he's a robot!" he exclaimed. "Have you heard the latest? He wants us to cut down on art lessons and do more math and English instead, so he can save money on materials!"

Neil and Chris were outraged.

"Who told you that?" Neil asked.

Hasheem shrugged. "One of the kids overheard him talking to Smiler. It's all over the school!"

"It's just the kind of thing he'd do," Neil agreed, wondering what other ideas Mr. Grundy might come up with to save money at the Meadowbank School. . . .

"It's disgusting!" Emily raged. "He can't do it!"

"We've got to stop him, that's for sure," Neil said urgently. "Mr. Grundy isn't going to get away with this!"

"What are we going to do then?" Chris asked.

It was the end of the school day, and Neil and Chris had met up with Emily in the playground near the bike stands. They were still stunned by what had happened at the end of the afternoon, just before the final bell. A letter had been handed out to every student for their parents. Mr. Grundy was "pleased to inform parents that from now on classroom pets were no longer appropriate." The rabbits, hamsters, guinea pigs, and gerbils that were already in the school would be "disposed of" at the earliest opportunity.

"He should leave our animals alone!" Emily said angrily. "Why does he want to get rid of them?"

"To save money, I suppose," Neil muttered. The decision to get rid of the animals had come as a complete shock to the whole school, and some of the younger children had burst into tears when they were told. Although it was ten minutes since the bell, there were still some groups of children hanging around outside discussing this latest development.

"Well, it's just not right!" Emily declared passionately. "I bet the other teachers don't like it."

Just at that moment Mr. Hamley emerged from the school building staggering under the weight of four bags bulging with tests to be marked. Emily charged across the playground toward him. Neil and Chris followed behind her.

"Mr. Hamley!" Emily said breathlessly. "Do *you* think Mr. Grundy should take our animals away?"

Mr. Hamley frowned. "It's not up to me, I'm afraid, Emily," he said stiffly.

"But the animals are important," Emily went on. "Some of the children aren't allowed to have pets at home, and keeping them in class is the only chance they get to be around animals. *And* we learn about them, too."

"Well, we're all pretty attached to Tom and Jerry," he admitted reluctantly. Tom and Jerry were the gerbils that belonged to Mr. Hamley's class. "But it's Mr. Grundy's decision."

"Maybe he'll change his mind when he sees how upset everyone is," Neil suggested.

But Mr. Hamley shook his head. "I really can't discuss this," he said shortly. "I'm on my way home, and you should be, too."

"I'll be by in a little while to pick up Dotty," Neil reminded him.

Mr. Hamley nodded and gave a fleeting smile, then hurried off toward the school gates.

"He's much nicer when he's with Dotty," Emily muttered.

"Well, I suppose he feels a little awkward," Chris said. "He can't really side with us against Mr. Grundy, can he?"

"What are we going to do?" Emily asked, her voice full of despair.

Neil smiled. "I've got an idea," he said triumphantly. "And it's something that's going to make Grumpy Grundy *really* sit up and take notice!"

CHAPTER THREE

"I think a petition is a *brilliant* idea!" Emily said enthusiastically as she, Neil, and Sam walked up to the Hamleys's front door. Neil had gone home to get Sam, and Emily had decided to come with him to walk Dotty. "It's one of the best ideas you've ever had!"

"Thanks," Neil said modestly. "Just call me a genius!"

Emily made a face at him. "A show-off is more like it! I hope we get lots of signatures!"

"Yeah, that'll show Mr. Grundy we mean business and —" Neil broke off hastily as Mr. Hamley opened the door. "Hello, sir." Neil had to raise his voice to be heard above the baby crying loudly inside the house. "Is Dotty ready for her walk?"

Mr. Hamley nodded, looking distracted. He disappeared down the hall and came back with Dotty bounding alongside him on her leash.

"Hello, girl." Neil patted the dalmatian as she jumped up at him, wagging her tail furiously.

"Down, Dotty," Mr. Hamley snapped. "Don't take her too far, will you? I don't want her tired out." And he shut the door abruptly.

"Well!" Emily exclaimed as they went down the path with the two dogs. "He didn't even say thank you!"

"I think Mr. Hamley's got more important things to worry about," Neil said with a grin. "Did you hear the baby? It didn't stop crying the whole time we were there!"

"He did look pretty wound up," Emily admitted. She giggled as Dotty, who was now trotting alongside Sam, turned and gave the collie's ear a friendly nip. Sam was too well-trained to do the same back, but he wagged his tail hard in response. "Dotty seems happy enough, anyway!"

Neil agreed. Then he frowned. "I just hope Mr. Hamley realizes what he's taken on. Puppies can be a lot of hard work."

"As long as Dotty doesn't have one hundred and one dalmatians!" Emily doubled over with laughter at her own joke, and Neil grinned.

"I think we ought to figure out what we're going to do about the petition," he said as they left Compton behind and walked out into the countryside. "Mr.

Grundy's a fast worker. He'll have the classroom animals out before we know it."

Emily nodded. "We'd better do it tonight. What should it say?"

"Something like: 'Save Our Pets! We want Meadowbank School to keep our classroom animals to help our education'?" Neil suggested. "And then plenty of room for signatures underneath that. We're going to need a lot of copies."

"We'd better get to work as soon as we get in," Emily said. "Do you think we could get some of the parents to sign it?"

"Yes, I think we can!" Neil said, rumpling Sam's coat affectionately before letting him off his leash. Emily let Dotty loose, too, and the two dogs trotted off across the field, teasing each other with playful barks. "And we should start with Mom and Dad — Sarah's really upset about it."

Emily smirked. "Mr. Grundy's going to be *so* mad when he finds out!"

Neil shrugged. "He's usually in a bad mood anyway, so it won't make much difference."

They stayed in the field for about fifteen minutes exercising the dogs. Neil kept a close watch on both Dotty and Sam as they chased each other in circles, enjoying each other's company. It took him a while to persuade Dotty that it was time to go home, but eventually he got her leash on and they all headed back to Mr. Hamley's house.

Neil's teacher was looking marginally less stressed when he opened the door. The baby had stopped crying and Mr. Hamley had a big mug of tea in his hands. This time he thanked them quite warmly for taking Dotty out, and Neil arranged to come for her again on Wednesday after school. He felt a little guilty about leaving his dad to run the kennel single-handedly, but he couldn't let Mr. Hamley and Dotty down — not with a brood of little Dotties on the way.

"How was the barking-mad dalmatian?" Carole Parker asked as Neil, Emily, and Sam clattered into the kitchen. She was sitting at the table with Sarah, who was drawing a picture, crayons spread out around her.

"She's fine." Neil emptied Sam's bowl and filled it with fresh water. The collie wagged his tail gratefully and took a long drink. "Mr. Hamley seems more worried than she is!"

"How's your hand, Mom?" Emily asked.

Carole shrugged. "Not too bad. I haven't been able to do anything today, though."

"Never mind," Neil said quickly. "You'll be OK again soon." Carole didn't say anything, but Neil thought she looked anxious. He could guess why his mom was feeling bad, though. With Kate away and Carole out of action, Bob Parker was swamped with work.

"Did you read Mr. Grundy's letter about the classroom animals, Mom?" Emily asked. "Don't you think it *stinks*?"

"I think it's horrible," Sarah said huffily. "I know the school pets aren't as smart as Fudge, but why does he want to get rid of them?"

Neil grinned. Fudge was Sarah's hamster, and according to her, he was the most intelligent hamster who had ever lived, though no one else in the family had seen any sign of it.

"He's trying to save the school some money," Neil replied. "But I don't think the animals cost that much to keep, anyway."

"Mr. Grundy does seem to have a great talent for getting people upset," Carole Parker agreed, glancing at the letter again.

"That's why we've started a petition!" Emily told their mother exactly what they were planning. Carole looked interested. "Well, there's certainly no harm in making your views known," she said. "As long as you go about it properly and peacefully."

"It won't be peaceful with Em around!" Neil said, and Emily stuck her tongue out at him. "Does Dad need a hand, Mom?"

"I'm sure he does." Carole's smile disappeared. "Why don't you go and see?"

Neil checked on Sam, who was already dozing under the kitchen table, then he went over to the kennels.

His father was in Kennel Block One, just coming out of Duke's pen. Neil felt his heart skip a beat as he approached the pen, but Duke was looking subdued, gulping down the food Bob had just given him. Bob had taken sole responsibility for Duke's care, and no one else was allowed in the pen.

"Do you need a hand, Dad?"

Duke raised his head at the sound of Neil's voice and stared miserably at him through the fence. Neil couldn't help feeling sorry for the dog. "Hello, boy," he said softly, but Duke didn't respond any further. He turned his back on Neil and went through the door that led to the outdoor run.

"That's one miserable dog," Bob Parker remarked as he unlocked the next pen. "I wish I knew why he is the way he is."

"Do you think it's the Carters's fault?" Neil asked sadly. He hated to see any dog in pain — physical or mental.

"We'll soon find out when they get back on Saturday morning," Bob said grimly. "Do you want to feed Buttons for me?"

"Sure!" Neil said, cheering up. Buttons was a friendly little black-and-white dog, bright-eyed and lively. Although she had found it difficult to settle in on her first visit to King Street, she was now completely at home whenever she visited. She launched herself at Neil, barking a welcome as he went into the pen.

"Good girl!" Neil stroked her, then put the bowl down. Buttons immediately sat down and gobbled up the food, her tail still wagging furiously.

"How's Dotty?" Bob asked as Neil came out of Buttons's pen.

"Fighting fit!" Neil said with a grin.

"That's good news." Bob, who was looking exhausted, yawned and rubbed his eyes. "I'm beat. I'd really appreciate it if you and Emily could help out with walking the dogs before school tomorrow."

"I'll get up a little bit earlier," Neil promised, trying hard to sound enthusiastic. It was important that the dogs' routine was not disturbed, even while the kennel was shorthanded, and Neil was determined that the dogs would not suffer. Anyway, it was only for a few days until his mother and Kate were back at work.

"Ow!" Carole Parker complained, moving her bandaged hand gingerly to and fro. "It still hurts."

Bob finished off his toast and got up from the breakfast table. "You'd better rest it again today, love. I can manage."

Carole looked upset. "I can still do the paperwork . . ." she began.

But Bob shook his head. "Be sensible, Carole. You won't be able to hold a pen properly."

"I can use the computer, though," Carole argued, looking determined.

Neil, who was hurriedly wolfing down some cereal after taking a few of the dogs for a run, wondered why his mother's hand didn't seem to be getting any better. The injury must have been even worse than he'd thought.

"Hurry up, you slowpokes!" Emily burst into the kitchen, waving a stack of papers in one hand. "We've got to get to school early to start collecting signatures for our petition!"

"Ah, yes, the famous petition!" Bob remarked, pulling his coat on. "Are you going to let us sign it?"

"Sure!" Emily said, proudly. "You'll be the first — well, after me and Neil, of course!"

"I want to sign it, too!" Sarah insisted.

Emily gave one of the sheets she was holding to her father. She and Neil had spent hours on the computer the previous night making the petition look as professional as possible. The heading was SAVE OUR PETS! in big black letters, and the space for signatures had been neatly divided up into separate boxes for names and addresses.

Bob signed it quickly, then passed the sheet to Carole, who, as he had predicted, found it a real struggle to write. By the time Sarah had laboriously printed out her full name in capital letters, Emily was dancing impatiently from one foot to the other.

"Come *on,* we've got to go!"

Neil quickly said good-bye to Sam, and Bob ushered all of them out of the house and into the Range Rover. Neil crammed his bike into the back and jumped inside. He didn't usually like arriving at school with his sisters, but today was a special occasion. He and Emily needed to start collecting signatures together.

"Good luck!" their mother called after them.

They got to school well before the morning bell. There were plenty of people around, including a circle of parents at the school gates.

"Did you get the petition drawn up?" Chris asked eagerly, running over to meet them.

Emily nodded and pulled the pile of papers out of her bag. "We need to get as many signatures as we can before the bell rings," she said urgently.

Chris grinned. "I've already got a bunch of people lined up!" He pointed at a small group of students from Mr. Hamley's class, including Hasheem, who were hanging around by the bike stands. "They're all waiting to sign!"

Neil, Emily, and Chris headed over to them.

"Come on," said Hasheem cheerfully. "Where's this petition?"

Neil grabbed one of the printed sheets from Emily and gave it to him.

"I'll ask some of the other kids," Emily decided.

"No need for that," Hasheem said, signing his name with a flourish. He cupped both hands around his mouth and yelled: "If you want to keep your school pets, come and sign our petition! Guaranteed to make Mr. Grundy sit up and take notice!"

"Thanks, Hasheem!" Neil said as kids began to hurry over to see what was going on. "Who needs a loudspeaker system with you around?"

Suddenly everyone in the playground seemed to want to sign the petition. Neil, Emily, and Chris were swamped on all sides and were kept busy handing out the sheets of paper.

"We should try to get some parents' signatures, too, before the bell," Emily muttered to Neil.

"I'll go and ask them." Neil prepared to shoulder

his way out of the mass of children milling around, but it was too late. A tall, stiff figure was striding toward them, looking very angry indeed.

"Can somebody please tell me *what* is going on here?"

Neil's heart sank. It was Mr. Grundy.

CHAPTER FOUR

"**W**ell?" Mr. Grundy sat behind the large, daunting desk in his office, the crumpled pages of the petition in front of him. "Would one of you like to explain the meaning of that *disgusting* scene in the playground this morning?"

Neil, Emily, and Chris sat on metal chairs in front of the desk and shuddered.

Neil wondered what the principal was expecting them to say. After all, it was obvious what they had been doing. "We were collecting signatures, Mr. Grundy," he said, "for our petition."

"I can see that!" Mr. Grundy snapped. "You come to school to work, not to get involved in foolish escapades like this," he went on sternly. "I will be writing to your parents —"

"Our parents signed the petition, sir," Neil pointed out.

Mr. Grundy glared at him. "We'll have no more of this nonsense in my school." He picked up the petition, ripped the papers in half, and threw them into the wastebasket.

Emily gasped, outraged. "But we just want to keep our animals! No one wants to get rid of them except you —"

"That's enough!" Mr. Grundy looked so fierce that Neil couldn't help feeling a little afraid of him. "I expect you to stay in and do extra math during the morning break. I will supervise you *personally.*"

"What a creep!" Emily said indignantly when they were dismissed. "He didn't even *bother* to listen to what we had to say!"

"All that hard work for nothing!" Chris groaned.

"Never mind," Neil said. "We can easily print up some more sheets."

"But he won't let us collect signatures in school!" Emily wailed, frustrated.

Neil grinned. "OK, so we're not allowed to collect signatures *in* school. But he can't stop us from doing it *outside,* can he?"

Chris smiled. "Well, it's sneaky, but it might work."

"He'll probably have us arrested!" Emily laughed.

"Let's come back tomorrow morning with a new petition and collect signatures outside the school gates," Neil said in a determined voice. "Grumpy

Grundy might think he's beaten us, but we're not finished yet."

"I have a note to read to you from Mr. Grundy," Mr. Hamley announced to his class just before lunchtime.

Neil nudged Hasheem. "Guess what this is about," he whispered.

Mr. Hamley cleared his throat. *"There will be no change in the decision regarding the school pets,"* he read out loud, with a glance at the gerbils' cage in the corner of the classroom. Tom and Jerry were asleep, curled up together in a furry ball, blissfully unaware of their impending fate. *"They will be removed at the end of the week."*

The whole class began to mutter, and Neil frowned. That meant they only had three days left to change the principal's mind. *If* they could change his mind.

"Put your work away, please," called Mr. Hamley as the bell for lunchtime rang out. At the same time he hastily put up his hand to smother a yawn, and Neil noticed again how tired he was looking. He also couldn't help smiling as he saw that Mr. Hamley was wearing mismatched socks, one navy blue and one black. With the teacher's heavy workload, and Dotty and the new baby to cope with, it was no wonder that he seemed distracted.

"Do you really think the petition is going to do any good?" Chris asked as he and Neil met up in the hall and went to lunch. The cafeteria was a low-roofed but spacious extension, which had been added onto the side of the two-story school building.

"Not if it's just us kids who are signing it," Neil replied above the din of clattering plates and multiple conversations. "Grumpy won't pay any attention to us. But if we can get some of the parents involved . . ."

"Yeah, you're right!" Chris agreed. "This one needs parent power. I bet lots of them are as fed up with Mr. Grundy as we are."

Hasheem was already in the food line when Neil and Chris joined it. He saw them and made gagging noises.

"Thanks a lot!" Neil said. "I thought you were a friend!"

"Not you — the food!" Hasheem groaned. "Haven't you seen it? It's gross!"

Neil and Chris stood on tiptoe and stared over the heads of the people in front of them. They could see a meat loaf that looked rock-hard, some lumpy mashed potatoes, and a large, watery bowl of gray stuff.

"That's disgusting!" Chris said, making a face. "That gray thing looks like a chemistry experiment!"

Neil wondered what had happened. Their school

lunches were usually pretty good, although they weren't always very exciting.

"Meat loaf or cheese-and-onion quiche?" asked the lunch lady as the three boys reached the counter.

"Oh, thanks for letting us know what they are," Hasheem said. "It's kind of impossible to tell."

"We'll have less of your smart-aleck comments, thank you, Hasheem Lindon!" said the lunch lady, but only halfheartedly.

"What happened to the food?" Hasheem went on. "You know, the stuff we could actually eat?"

"We've changed to a different caterer," the lunch-lady said shortly, picking up a serving spoon.

"Mr. Grundy!" Neil snapped at the others. "I bet he's changed the caterers to save money!"

The boys took their plates over to an empty table and sat down.

"Watch your teeth on the cheese-and-onion quiche!" Neil advised the others, once he'd managed to saw through the pastry.

Hasheem took a taste of the mashed potatoes and almost spat it out again.

"More lumps than mash!" he spluttered.

"Grundy's done it again," Neil sighed. "Everyone at Meadowbank School is going to be up in arms over this."

When classes began again after lunch, some of the children in Neil's class complained to Mr. Hamley about the school lunches. Neil didn't because he felt sorry for the exhausted teacher. But all through the afternoon he sensed that a dark cloud of resentment was hanging over the school because everyone was fed up with Mr. Grundy's behavior. It really depressed Neil. Meadowbank had always been such a happy school, and he'd enjoyed going there — well, as much as anyone could enjoy school, anyway. Now he was relieved when the bell rang and he could go home.

"Don't forget to bring some more petition sheets tomorrow!" Chris called after Neil as he rode his bike toward his house.

Neil waved and headed off on his own bike toward

King Street Kennels, where Sam rushed to meet him. Neil knelt down and made a huge fuss over the collie, reassuring Sam, as he always did, that he'd missed him enormously while he was at school.

His mother was in the kitchen, and she looked up as Neil came in. "Hi, how was your day?"

"Mr. Grundy ripped up our petition and our school lunch was disgusting," Neil replied. "Aside from that, it was great."

Carole looked sympathetic as Neil explained exactly what had happened. "I think Mr. Grundy's going a little too far," she remarked. "But he *is* new. Maybe he'll calm down soon."

Neil wasn't very hopeful. "Are you feeling better, Mom?" he asked, looking at her bandaged hand.

Carole shrugged. "I'm all right. Your dad's gone to pick up the girls, and then he's going to buy some supplies."

Neil couldn't help noticing that she changed the subject pretty quickly. "For the dogs?" he asked.

"No, for us!" Carole grinned ruefully. "I haven't been able to go shopping."

"OK, I'll start walking the dogs before Dad gets back," Neil offered. "I was hoping I might have time to go and see Jake tonight, though." Neil couldn't wait for Jake to move to King Street Kennels, and he loved visiting the perky pup at Old Mill Farm.

"That shouldn't be a problem," his mother said.

"Great!" Neil knelt down and put his arm around Sam's neck. "Do you want to go and see Jake, boy?"

Sam's bright, alert eyes lit up even more, and he gave a short, sharp bark.

"I think that means yes!" Neil grinned. "Are you ready for a walk, Sam?"

Sam barked again and looked around for his leash. He spotted it hanging over a chair and went to retrieve it.

"Why don't you come with us, Mom?" Neil suggested. "Some fresh air might do you good."

"No, I don't think so," Carole said quickly.

"Oh, come on, Mom," Neil urged her. "We'll take Buttons and Robbie — they love going for walks with Sam." Robbie was a golden Labrador that was on his first visit to the kennel while his owner was in the hospital.

Carole was shaking her head even before Neil had finished speaking. "I said no, Neil," she snapped. "Now get a move on if you're going out."

Neil didn't say anything else. He and Sam went out of the house and over to Kennel Block One to get the dogs, but all the time Neil was thinking hard. There was definitely something wrong with his mother, and it wasn't just the injury to her hand. She had overreacted badly to his suggestion that she come with him to walk the dogs. At the moment Carole didn't seem like the calm, capable woman Neil knew, and he suspected that she hadn't been back to the kennel blocks since Duke had bitten her.

A sudden thought hit him hard, and he stopped, dismayed, to consider its implications. Had his mother lost her nerve with dogs?

CHAPTER FIVE

"Mom?" Neil hung around deliberately after breakfast the next day to have a quiet word with his mother, refusing a ride to school from his father who had gone off earlier with Emily and Sarah. Emily hadn't been too pleased because they were supposed to be collecting signatures for the petition again that morning. But Neil felt that he had to do something right away if his suspicions about his mother were true. He had slept poorly the night before, wondering if he was right, and, if he was, what it would mean for King Street Kennels.

"You'd better hurry or you'll be late," Carole remarked as she cleared the breakfast dishes.

It seemed to Neil that she was avoiding his gaze.

"Mom . . . about what happened with Duke," he began in a determined voice.

"That's over and done with." Carole turned away from Neil so that he couldn't see her face, but he was sure that he was right. His mother *had* lost her nerve with dogs.

Neil wondered if the injury to her hand was still as bad as she claimed, or if she was pretending it was still painful so she could avoid the kennel. "All right, so when are you going to start helping out with the dogs again?"

His mother took a deep breath before replying. "When my hand's a little better, Neil. Anyway, Kate should be back on Monday, and then things will get easier."

"They say if you fall off a horse, you should get right back on again," Neil pointed out, his heart hammering with anxiety. He hated seeing his mother like this, but it made him realize just how much the attack had affected her.

"What do you mean?" Carole asked in a threatening tone.

Neil knew he ought to stop right there, but he couldn't. "Well, if the dogs are making you nervous now, you should start going into the kennel again."

Carole Parker controlled herself with a visible effort. "Neil, I'm fine, and I'll be back at work before you know it."

"Maybe if you talked to Dad —" Neil began.

"No," Carole said sharply. "And I don't want you bothering him, either. He's got enough on his plate at the moment."

"But —"

"I mean it, Neil."

He nodded reluctantly. He never argued with his mother when she spoke to him in that particular tone.

Neil went out of the house slowly. Well, he'd messed that up, hadn't he? He climbed onto his bike and pedaled off toward Compton, wondering what was going to happen next. His mother had always been completely involved in the kennel and she loved dogs as much as his father did. Neil didn't want to think about what the consequences would be if Carole decided she didn't want to work with dogs anymore.

"Hey, Neil!" Chris was bicycling furiously to meet him. "I thought we were supposed to get to school early to collect signatures? You're going about as fast as a snail with a limp!"

Neil blinked. He'd been so worried about his mom, he'd almost forgotten about the petition. "Sorry!"

The two boys raced to the school. By the time they got there, Emily was already surrounded by a huge crowd of children and parents outside the school gates, all busily signing the new petition.

"About time, too!" Emily snapped when Neil and Chris arrived. "I'm drowning in signatures!"

The two boys grabbed some sheets of paper and joined in. There was even more interest today than there had been before. Word had gotten around that the principal had ripped up the first petition, and now everyone was even more indignant.

"I really think Mr. Grundy should change his mind about this," said Mrs. Jones as she signed her name. Her daughter, Kathy, was in Neil's class.

"Maybe the PTA could make a formal protest," another mother suggested.

"Or we could complain to the chairman of the school board, that nice Mr. Bingham," said another.

Neil, Emily, and Chris shot one another looks of delight. This time Mr. Grundy wouldn't be able to ignore their petition, Neil thought triumphantly. Then his heart began to race as he looked up and saw the principal hurrying across the playground toward them. Mr. Grundy looked as if he was ready to explode with fury.

"Quick, grab all the sheets!" Neil said under his breath. They just about managed to get all of them back before Mr. Grundy reached the gate, and Emily flipped through them, counting under her breath.

"We've got nearly eleven pages!" she whispered to Neil and Chris.

Neil did a quick calculation. There was room for ten signatures on each page which meant they had collected more than one hundred signatures! That thought gave Neil the courage to stand up straight and meet Mr. Grundy's accusing glare.

"What is going on out here?" he asked tightly. "Didn't you hear the bell?"

"Here, sir." Neil took the sheets from Emily and handed them over to the principal. "We'd really like to keep the animals in our classrooms, and so would everyone who's signed our petition."

Mr. Grundy stared down at the sheets of paper as if he'd like to shred them into bits right there and then. But as Neil had guessed, he didn't dare while there were parents standing around watching.

"Well," he blustered, "we'll have to see about that."

"I hope you'll reconsider, Mr. Grundy," Mrs. Jones said. Some of the other parents murmured agreement. "My Kathy's really upset about it."

"I'll certainly . . . take into consideration your . . . heartfelt views," Mr. Grundy said coldly. "Now please make your way into school, all of you."

"We did it!" Emily whispered to Neil and Chris, as the principal walked away.

Neil shook his head. "Not quite. He hasn't changed his mind yet."

"He will!" Emily said confidently. "You wait and see!"

Chris gave Neil a thumbs-up sign as they went into their separate classrooms. "I think we've really made Grumpy sit up and take notice this time!"

Neil nodded, but as he went in to Mr. Hamley's classroom, he felt slightly uneasy. He couldn't help wondering what Mr. Grundy's next move would be.

"Hurry up, Neil," Mr. Hamley snapped. He was already at his desk, attendance book open. "We haven't got all day."

Neil looked at the teacher as he hurried over to his seat. Mr. Hamley looked worse than ever. His shirt hadn't been properly ironed, and he was yawning almost continuously as he took the attendance. Neil wondered if his teacher was getting any sleep at all. It certainly didn't look like it.

Neil couldn't help worrying about Dotty. He knew how much the Hamleys loved the dalmatian, but they had so much going on at the moment. He was concerned that Dotty wasn't getting the special care that a mother-to-be needed.

Still, he would be able to check on the dog himself when he went there to walk her again after school.

Nobody saw Mr. Grundy all day, and nothing was heard about the petition. But when the last bell rang that afternoon, Mr. Hamley handed out yet another letter from the principal for the class to take home to their parents. Neil wondered if Mr. Grundy had made a final decision about the fate of the school animals, but the letter turned out to be about something quite different.

"I am very concerned about the standards of dress in our school," Neil read aloud as he and Chris walked out into the playground. *"Many of the pupils are letting the school down by not making sure their uniforms are clean and tidy.*

"I will therefore be making weekly inspections to check that the pupils' hairstyles, clothes, and shoes are of an acceptable standard." Chris went on, sounding as pompous as old Grumpy Grundy himself. *"As part of this drive to raise standards, girls will not be permitted to wear pants to school next term."*

Neil raised his eyebrows. "Well, *that's* going to please Em," he began, and right at that moment Emily raced over to them, waving the letter.

"Have you *seen* this?"

Neil and Chris nodded.

"He can't do it!" Emily stormed. "It's against the law — at least, I think it is!"

"I don't think that'll bother Grumpy," Neil remarked. "He does what he likes!"

"We've got to do *something*!" Emily went on determinedly. "I think we should start another petition!"

"Hey, one petition at a time!" Neil said. "Let's sort out the school animals first."

"I'm going to tell Dad!" Emily raged as she saw their father's Range Rover pull up outside the school gates. "Mr. Grundy's got no right to do this!"

"Remind Dad that I'm going to walk Dotty, will you?" Neil shouted after her. "I'll get home as soon as I can."

He said good-bye to Chris and rode off to Mr. Hamley's house. Life was pretty hectic at the moment, Neil thought as he wheeled his bike up the Hamleys's sidewalk. In all the excitement about the petition and his concerns about Dotty and his mom, he'd almost forgotten that Duke's owners were returning on Saturday to pick up their dog. Neil wasn't looking forward to that at all.

He leaned his bike against the porch and rang the doorbell. There was no answer, though Neil could hear Dotty barking somewhere in the house. He wondered where Mr. Hamley had gone. If the teacher had to stay late at school, surely he would have said so. Or maybe Mr. Hamley had forgotten their arrangement, Neil thought, dismayed.

"Oh, Neil, sorry to keep you waiting." Mr. Hamley hurried up the sidewalk toward him, laden down with bags of books and papers. He fumbled for his key and pushed open the door. "Come in."

Neil blinked at the mess in the hallway in front of him. There were all sorts of things strewn around: baby toys, dog biscuits, and newspapers, among other things. Meanwhile, Dotty could be heard scrabbling frantically at the kitchen door and whining.

"I've had to shut Dotty in the kitchen." Mr. Hamley dropped his bags and hurried down the hallway. "Sorry about the mess," he apologized stiffly. "My wife had to go up to Manchester on Monday night. Her mother's ill. I had to rush home at lunchtime to let Dotty out."

"Oh, I'm sorry." Neil began to feel even more alarmed as he realized that Dotty had been left on her own all day. He knew that puppies could arrive up to five days early, and even though Dotty had just over a week to wait before the birth, something could still go wrong. Neil bit his lip. He knew he had to be careful because Mr. Hamley was his teacher, but he had to say *something*.

"Mr. Hamley," he began, but he didn't have time for anything more. The teacher opened the kitchen door, and Dotty shot out like a rocket, barking loudly.

She threw herself at her owner, and then dashed up to Neil, her brown eyes dancing with pleasure.

"Dotty, behave yourself!" Mr. Hamley gasped, grabbing the excited dog by her collar. Then he stiffened. "What's that yellow stuff around her mouth?"

Neil looked more closely. Now he could see that Dotty did indeed have bright-yellow marks around her jaws.

"Do you think she's got some kind of disease?" Mr. Hamley stared at Neil anxiously.

Neil looked again. "No, I don't think she's sick," he said, trying hard not to laugh. "Have you given her any curry recently?"

Mr. Hamley suddenly looked guilty. He hurried into the kitchen and Neil and Dotty followed him. The kitchen was also a mess. On the floor were a couple of foil takeout containers that were licked clean.

"I had takeout Indian food for dinner last night and I didn't get around to cleaning up," Mr. Hamley muttered "You're a bad girl, Dotty!"

Neil frowned. He wasn't finding the situation very funny now at all. The curry probably wouldn't hurt Dotty, but what if she had eaten something else that *might* have affected her? And anyway, in Dotty's present condition, she certainly shouldn't be left on her own.

"Mr. Hamley, is there anyone who can look after Dotty in the daytime?" he asked tentatively. "She really shouldn't be on her own right now."

"I'm well aware of that, thank you, Neil," Mr. Hamley snapped, turning red. "You can rest assured that I've made other arrangements starting tomorrow."

Neil couldn't help wondering what those arrangements were as he fastened Dotty's leash to her collar. He sighed inwardly as the dalmatian licked his hand and looked up into his face trustingly. Neil just hoped that Mr. Hamley knew what he was doing because if he didn't, Dotty and her soon-to-be-born puppies would be the ones to suffer.

CHAPTER SIX

When Neil arrived at King Street Kennels, his mother was in the office. She was at the computer typing with her good hand, and on the floor was a wire basket with a small black dog inside. The dog was long-haired and looked like a woolly teddy bear. He was shivering and whining pathetically, his large brown eyes fixed on Carole's face, but she wasn't paying much attention to him.

"Hey, who's this?" Neil asked, bending over the basket. The dog instantly shrank back into a corner, looking scared, so Neil let him sniff his hand. When the dog's tail began to wag cautiously, he scratched the top of his shaggy head. "Hello, boy!"

"Sergeant Moorhead brought him in," his mother

replied. "He was found wandering around downtown. Nobody claimed him."

"Poor thing." Neil put the basket on the desk, close to where his mother was sitting. She didn't flinch, but she didn't look at the little dog, either. Neil felt very depressed. He'd never seen his mother look so uninterested in a dog before, especially a stray. The little dog had begun to whine again as he stared hopefully up at Carole, obviously longing for some attention. "Is he going into the rescue center?"

Carole nodded. "I'm just adding his details to our records now. Do you want to give him a name?"

"How about Star?" Neil suggested. "He's sure to be a hit with anybody looking for a new puppy."

"OK."

"Star couldn't have been a stray for very long," Neil said after looking the dog over. "He's been well cared for."

Carole glanced over at the dog and her face softened. "He's a funny little thing, isn't he? Maybe he's just lost and his owner will claim him soon. We'd better ask Mike to check him over, though." Mike Turner was the local vet. "Take Star over to the rescue center, will you, Neil? Your father and Emily are preparing a pen for him."

"All right," Neil said, picking up Star. He wished his mother had shown the dog a little more attention, but at least she'd seemed touched by the dog's plight. That was a start.

Sam was asleep in his favorite place under the hedge at the bottom of the garden, but he shook himself awake and raced up to Neil, barking a greeting. At the same time Bob, Emily, and Sarah came out of the rescue center.

"Quiet, Sam!" Neil ordered when he saw that Star was looking agitated again. "Sit!"

Sam immediately stopped barking and dropped onto his haunches. Then Neil lowered the basket and let Star and the collie sniff each other cautiously.

"Isn't he *gorgeous*?" Emily called. "I saw him when Sergeant Moorhead brought him in."

"I named him Star," Neil told her. "Is there a pen ready for him, Dad?"

Bob nodded and hurried off toward Kennel Block One, with Sarah following right behind him. Neil noticed how tired his father was looking and he wondered yet again if he ought to talk to him about his mom.

He turned to Emily and said, "Have you noticed anything strange about Mom?"

"Strange?" Emily looked puzzled. "What do you mean?"

Neil quickly explained and Emily's eyes widened. "But Mom loves dogs!" she exclaimed.

"I know. And maybe she'll get over it soon . . ." Neil tried to sound as if he believed it himself. "She told me not to talk to Dad about it, but I was wondering if I should."

Emily frowned. "He's really busy right now. Maybe you should wait a few days until Kate gets back next week. That'll give Mom some time to get more . . . normal."

"Yeah, you're probably right."

Star began whining again as Neil carried him into the rescue center and he picked up the scents of the other dogs. There were only two other strays at the moment, a Jack Russell named Rufus and a yappy brown dog named Lily. Both of them hurried over to take a look at the new arrival.

Neil took Star into an empty pen. He opened up the basket, but the little dog was so nervous at first that he refused to come out. Then, at last, he stepped out very cautiously and sniffed his way around the pen. That didn't seem to reassure him much though, because then he slumped down in a corner, still looking miserable.

"Poor old Star," Neil said sympathetically, ruffling the dog's silky ears. He was a nervous animal anyway, and if he had been accidentally separated from his owner, he must have gone through a very traumatic experience. It was a pity his mother hadn't shown the dog more interest, Neil thought. He was frustrated because Star seemed to like his mother. Maybe a gentle, timid dog like Star was the way to rebuild his mother's confidence with dogs.

Looking down at the sweet-natured, frightened little dog, Neil had an idea about how to help his mom. He locked up Star's pen and raced back to the house. Bob and Emily were now cleaning out Kennel Block Two, with Sarah close by. Carole was still in the office, so Neil was able to get what he needed without being seen. Then he hurried right back to Star.

"Good boy!" he said soothingly as he went into the pen. "Look what I've got for you."

Neil had sneaked into his parents' bedroom and picked up a favorite sweatshirt of his mother's. He held it out to Star. The dog sniffed it, then began to whine and paw at it. Neil let Star smell the sweatshirt for a few more seconds. Then he pulled a small piece of chicken he had grabbed from the fridge and gave it to the dog. Star gobbled it down eagerly.

"Good boy," Neil said again. He didn't know if his plan would work. He was hoping that Star would associate his mother's scent with the particularly tasty treat and be even more friendly toward her — maybe even encouraging her to go into the pen. It was a bit of a long shot, Neil knew, but he had to try something.

The next morning Neil and Emily hurried out before anyone else was up and went through the same exact routine several times with Star. Neil had told his sister about his plan and she was eager to see for herself whether it would work or not. Star had already caught on to this new game and was waiting excitedly for his treats as soon as he recognized the scent of the sweatshirt.

"Good dog!" Neil said, feeling very pleased as he stroked Star's shaggy little body.

"He's clever, isn't he?" Emily remarked, holding out her hand for Star to lick. "But how are you going to get Mom to come and see him if she's avoiding the dogs?"

"I'm working on it," Neil said.

After breakfast it was time for school and Neil rode off to meet Chris as usual.

"Do you think Mr. Grundy will tell us what he's de-

cided about the school pets today?" Chris asked as
they rode into Compton.

Neil frowned. "I don't know. Emily's convinced he's
going to back down, but I just can't see Grumpy giving in so easily. I wouldn't be surprised if we turned
up one morning and all the pets were gone! That's
exactly how Grumpy operates."

"Maybe we ought to start a petition to get rid of
him!" Chris suggested as they went into the playground.

"Well, we'd probably get *thousands* of signatures if
we did!" Neil said with a grin.

As the two boys locked up their bikes, Mr. Hamley
hurried through the school gates, weighed down
with bags as usual.

"Smiler's late, isn't he?" Chris remarked. "He's
usually here much earlier than this."

Neil didn't say anything. He suspected that the
teacher wasn't coping very well with his wife away,
but he didn't want to broadcast Mr. Hamley's prob-
lems around the school. He just hoped that Mr. Hamley had Dotty properly settled in, wherever he had
left her.

The bell rang and Mr. Hamley broke into an awkward run, impeded by the heavy bags he was carrying. Suddenly the handle of one of the bags broke
and books and folders spilled out onto the ground.
Neil and Chris immediately dashed over to help.

"Thanks, boys," Mr. Hamley said gratefully as they

helped him gather his belongings. Neil also picked up a can of dog food, which Mr. Hamley snatched from him and stuffed into one of the other bags. He looked embarrassed, Neil thought curiously. But why? Maybe he didn't want them to know that he was late because he'd been shopping before school. From Mr. Hamley's tense expression, Neil thought it was probably wise to keep quiet, so he walked straight to class in silence.

"Hey!" Hasheem nudged Neil as Mr. Hamley's students settled themselves down, ready for attendance. "What's up with old Smiler today? He looks like he's got ants in his pants!"

Neil glanced over at the teacher. Mr. Hamley did look pretty jumpy. He was pacing up and down in front of the blackboard, looking as if his mind was miles away. Neil felt sorry for him, because he guessed the teacher must be worrying about Dotty, wherever she was.

All through the first half of the morning, Mr. Hamley seemed on edge. As soon as the bell for recess rang, he got up and called out impatiently, "Come on, hurry up and go outside please."

Neil was still putting his math books away when he happened to look across the classroom at his teacher. He was astonished to see Mr. Hamley look around furtively, then slip the can of dog food into his jacket pocket.

Neil's eyes almost popped out of his head as Mr.

Hamley briskly left the classroom. He hurried after him, bumping into Chris who was outside in the corridor.

"Hey!" Chris complained jokingly. "What's the rush?"

"Mr. Hamley's just put that can of dog food in his pocket!" Neil gasped.

"So?" Chris looked puzzled.

Neil didn't wait to explain further. He rushed after Mr. Hamley, dragging his friend with him. The teacher was heading for the stairs that led down to the ground floor of the school. They trailed Mr. Hamley down the corridor, past a couple of classrooms, including Emily's, and then past the gym.

"You realize we're going to get into big trouble if we're spotted," Chris complained as they cautiously followed the teacher around a corner. "We're not allowed to be in this end of the school."

"I know," Neil said. "But something's going on, and I think I know what . . ."

"Stalking a teacher is probably forbidden, too," Chris mumbled on.

Neil grabbed Chris's arm and they ducked out of sight behind a display case as Mr. Hamley stopped and went inside a room right at the end of the long corridor and closed the door quietly behind him.

"That's the boiler room!" Neil muttered.

"So what?" Chris said. "Maybe Mr. Hamley wants

to talk to Mr. Johnson." Mr. Johnson was the custodian at the Meadowbank School.

Neil shook his head. "I don't think so." He tiptoed to the door, with Chris behind him and then stopped.

Suddenly the door opened again before either of the boys had a chance to flee. Mr. Hamley was standing there glaring at them. "What are you two doing here?" he demanded furiously. "You know very well it's off-limits, and —"

He didn't have a chance to say any more. The very next second Dotty joyfully raced out of the room and flung herself at Neil, barking a welcome.

CHAPTER SEVEN

"**D**otty!" Mr. Hamley turned bright red and made a futile grab at the dalmatian's collar. Dotty dodged him, still barking, and dashed from Neil to Chris, jumping up at them in turn, her tail thrashing wildly from side to side.

"Dotty, be quiet!" Mr. Hamley gasped. He grabbed at the dalmatian again, and this time he managed to control her. He pulled Dotty back into the room, and Neil and Chris followed. It was warm and cozy in there because of the large boiler in one corner and the heating pipes running along the walls. Dotty's dog basket lay on the floor with a bowl of water next to it and a selection of rubber toys.

Neil glanced at Chris, who was still looking amazed. So *this* was where Mr. Hamley was keeping

66

Dotty! The teacher must have dropped her off early this morning before anyone else was around, and then gone back home to get his books. That explained why he was late.

"What are you two doing down here?" Mr. Hamley snapped, trying to sound authoritative. Dotty stared at him, her eyes bright with mischief. "You know this area is off-limits!"

"Sorry, sir," said Neil and Chris together.

Mr. Hamley sighed. "I might have known I couldn't keep Dotty a secret. Oh, well, it was worth a try."

"Won't the custodian find out anyway?" Neil asked.

"Mr. Johnson's been — er — helping me out," Mr. Hamley confessed. "He knows Dotty's here and he's been checking up on her while I'm teaching. But he's the only one who knows."

Meaning that Mr. Grundy didn't, Neil thought. "We won't tell anyone, sir," he said eagerly. "We could help you, too."

Mr. Hamley looked embarrassed again. "No, that wouldn't be right," he said shortly. "I'll just have to make other arrangements." He sighed. "The trouble is, there isn't really anywhere else I can leave Dotty, and my wife won't be back till next week."

"It really is better if Dotty stays with you, sir," Neil pointed out gently. "Moving her around too much will upset her."

Mr. Hamley cleared his throat as the bell for the end of break rang in the distance. "Yes, I can see that, Neil. Now you should go back to class."

Neil and Chris gave Dotty a final pat and then hurried out of the room.

"You guessed Dotty was in there, didn't you?" Chris whispered to Neil as they went back toward their classrooms.

"Mr. Hamley putting that can of dog food in his pocket kind of gave it away!" Neil grinned.

"Do you think he'll still keep Dotty there?"

Neil shrugged. "For the moment. He doesn't seem to have much choice, and her puppies aren't due for another week or so. Dotty ought to be at home for the birth, though. She might be unsettled if she's in a strange place."

"Let's hope Mr. Grundy doesn't find out. If he doesn't want hamsters and gerbils in school, he's not going to want a dog!"

"I know." Neil looked worried. If the principal found out what was going on, Mr. Hamley would be in serious trouble. He hoped that Dotty would behave herself while she was hidden and not give their secret away, but, of course, no one ever knew quite what Dotty would do next. . . .

Neil found it difficult to concentrate on his work for the rest of the day. He was on edge all the time, and he kept stopping every few minutes to listen for the sound of Dotty barking. The boiler room was right underneath Mr. Hamley's classroom, but Neil couldn't hear a thing. Dotty was probably asleep for most of the day anyway, so it looked like her hiding place would remain undiscovered, at least for the next few days.

As the homeroom bell rang, Neil wondered how Mr. Hamley was going to get Dotty out of the school again. Presumably the teacher would have to wait until everyone else had gone home before he smuggled her out. Neil wished there was something he could do to help, but he didn't want to push it. Mr. Hamley was obviously embarrassed enough after being caught by two pupils.

"I got yelled at about a million times by Mrs. Stewart!" Chris confessed as he and Neil rode their bikes home. "I just couldn't concentrate because I was thinking about Dotty."

"Me, too," Neil agreed. "I just hope Smiler gets her out of school safely tonight. It'd be just his luck to run into Mr. Grundy!"

"Speaking of Grundy," Chris went on, "isn't it about time he told us what he's going to do about the school pets? He's had nearly all week to think it over."

"Maybe he'll tell us tomorrow. It's Friday and I'll bet he'll want it sorted out by the weekend."

"Or maybe he thinks if he keeps quiet, we'll forget about it," Chris suggested.

"With Em around? No chance!" Neil laughed. "See you tomorrow."

When Neil arrived home, no one was there except Sam, who jumped up to greet him, and his mother, who was in the office, again at the computer.

She was typing swiftly with both hands, but stopped abruptly as Neil walked in. "Hello, Neil. Have a good day?"

"OK." Neil had already decided not to say anything about Dotty being kept at school. It was Mr. Hamley's secret, not his. "How's Star?"

"Your father said he seems better today." Carole began to type again, but one-handed this time.

Neil's heart sank. His mother's hand was obviously getting better, even if she didn't want to admit it. How much longer could she keep this up?

"Mike should be here soon to check him out," she went on.

"I'll go and see Star now," Neil decided. "Do you want to come with me, Mom?"

Carole shook her head. "I want to get this paperwork finished."

Neil didn't argue because he knew it wouldn't do any good. He popped into the house, got his mother's sweatshirt from upstairs and some chunky ham slices from the fridge, and went to Star's pen.

The little dog had been sleeping, but he uncurled himself and rushed across the pen on his short, stumpy legs, his tail wagging from side to side.

"Here, boy!" Neil murmured, holding out the sweatshirt. Star sniffed at it and then barked expectantly, his eyes locking onto the ham in Neil's hand. Neil handed it over and Star gulped it down.

"Good dog!" Neil scratched Star's woolly coat, pleased that his plan was working so well, although it wouldn't be any use unless he could bring Star and his mother together. That was going to be difficult, unless somehow he could get his mother over to the rescue center. . . .

"Hi, Neil!" Mike Turner walked into the rescue center, carrying his medical bag. He was often called in at the kennel and knew the Parker family very well. "How's the new arrival?"

"He's a great little dog," Neil said as Mike let himself into the pen. "He was a little nervous yesterday, but he's calmed down now."

"I'd better let *him* check *me* out first, then!" Mike waited patiently for Star to sniff at him cautiously, then he knelt down to look him over. Star submitted patiently to the examination. "He's been very well cared for," he said at last. "That shaggy coat of his would be a lot more tangled if he'd been a stray for any length of time."

"We're hoping his owners are looking for him," Neil began, then he broke off as his mother appeared unexpectedly in the doorway.

"Mike?" Carole's voice sounded a little shaky to Neil as she walked into the rescue center. "Janice just called." Janice was Mike's receptionist at the animal hospital. "Your cell phone is switched off. She said you should go over to Longbrook Farm when you've finished here. There's a problem with one of the cows."

"Thanks, Carole." Mike smiled at her, then glanced at Star. "Hey, boy, what's the matter with you?"

Star had smelled Carole Parker now and had pulled away from the vet. He raced up to the wire fence and pawed at it, whining loudly, his brown eyes shining underneath his curtain of long hair.

"I think you've got an admirer, Carole!" Mike said teasingly, and Neil was thrilled to see that his mother couldn't help smiling. She looked down at the excited dog and Neil held his breath. Then very slowly Carole bent down and put her good hand to the wire fence. Star strained to lick her fingers, and although Carole flinched slightly, Neil was very happy to see that she didn't pull away. Then she stroked the dog's head and Star looked up at her adoringly.

"I'd better get over to the farm," Mike said.

Neil was feeling very proud of himself. Carole gave Star another pat and then followed Mike out. His plan was working! He was becoming increasingly hopeful now that, with Star's help, his mother would soon be back to normal.

Bob and the girls arrived home just as Mike was leaving.

"Where've you been — Timbuktu?" Neil remarked. "I got home ages ago!"

Emily rolled her eyes. "Sarah forgot her reading book and we had to turn around and go back to school to get it!"

"*Sor-ree!*" Sarah said with dignity. "I'm trying to teach Fudge to read, and that's the book we're up to!"

"Speaking of hamsters," Mike remarked, "I'll be coming to your school tomorrow to pick up the pets."

Neil and Emily stared at him.

"*What?*" Emily gasped.

Mile looked puzzled. "I thought you all knew. Your principal called me this afternoon and asked me if I could — well — 'dispose of them' are actually the words he used."

"That horrible creep!" Emily burst out. "He didn't even tell us what he was planning!"

"I suppose he was just going to have the animals taken away and not tell us till it was all over!" Neil exclaimed angrily. "Typical Grumpy!"

Mike frowned. "I persuaded him to let me try to find homes for them. But I didn't realize he was going behind everyone's back."

"It's not your fault, Mike," Bob pointed out.

"Well, the whole thing does seem unfair to the kids — I know they've put a lot of work into looking after those animals," Mike said grimly.

As the vet went out, Neil turned to Emily. "Well, that's that, then," he said gloomily. "Mr. Grundy's got the better of us once and for all."

"Not quite!" Emily retorted. She marched over to the telephone, a determined look on her face. "I think it's time we let Jake Fielding at the *Compton News* know about this!"

"So Emily called the *Compton News* last night and spoke to Jake Fielding and he's coming over to do a story about the school pets this morning!" Neil told Chris triumphantly as they rode their bikes into the playground. Jake Fielding, a young photographer with the local newspaper, had covered stories at King Street Kennels several times. "That'll show Mr. Grundy we mean business!"

"Good one!" Chris said, pleased. "I can't believe Grumpy was just going to get rid of the animals!"

Neil shrugged. "That's what Grundy's like, though, isn't it? I mean, he really doesn't care what we think."

Hasheem caught the end of Neil's sentence and grinned. "What's he done now?"

"Wait till you hear this!" Neil said.

The news about Mr. Grundy was all over the school in no time. Everyone was disgusted about his plans and by the time Neil got to his classroom, several of his friends were already complaining loudly to Mr. Hamley. The teacher was looking a little distracted.

"Ah, Neil." Mr. Hamley hurried over as soon as he saw him. "I — er — brought Dotty in early this morning and I haven't had a chance to check up on her since," he said in a low voice. "So I was wondering . . ."

"Do you want me to go and see her?" Neil asked in a whisper.

Mr. Hamley nodded gratefully and Neil quietly slipped out of the classroom. There was no one around as he hurried down to the boiler room. When he pulled the door open, Dotty, who had been curled up in her basket looking sleepy, immediately leaped up to meet him.

"Hello, Spotty Dotty!" Neil whispered, stroking the dog's soft, gleaming coat. Dotty snuggled lovingly up against him, but Neil didn't dare stay too long. He gave Dotty a final caress, then went over to the door.

Dotty followed him.

"No, Dotty!" Neil said sternly. "Basket!"

Dotty whined, looking sad, but she climbed in and curled up again. Neil suddenly heard footsteps and quickly left the room.

"What are you doing in there, Neil Parker!"

The loud, accusing voice from the other end of the corridor made Neil almost jump out of his skin. He turned to see Mr. Grundy advancing furiously toward him.

"Mr. Hamley sent me to look for the custodian, sir." Neil prayed desperately that Dotty wouldn't start barking at the sound of his voice. "There's something wrong with the radiator in our classroom."

"I see." Mr. Grundy looked marginally less angry. "I'm looking for Mr. Johnson myself. Is he in there?" And the principal gestured toward the boiler room.

"No, sir," Neil answered, his heart thumping so loudly he was sure Grumpy must be able to hear it.

"Well, go straight back to class, please," said Mr. Grundy curtly, and he went off down the corridor.

Shaking with relief, Neil hurried back upstairs to the classroom. That had been too close a call for his liking.

"Was everything all right, Neil?" Mr. Hamley

asked as the class lined up for assembly. Neil nodded. He didn't see any point in worrying the teacher even further by telling him what had happened. He joined the end of the line and followed the rest of his class into the auditorium.

The auditorium was large, but with the whole school in there, sitting in rows, there was hardly any space to move. Mr. Grundy was already in there, pacing up and down on the low platform that stood at one end of the room. Neil's class was last to go in, and the principal glared at them for keeping him waiting.

"Before we start our assembly," Mr. Grundy began loudly, staring down at the rows of children seated in front of him, "I want to clear up the matter of the school pets."

Neil turned around to glance at Chris. Obviously the principal had been forced into this announcement because he'd been found out. Neil was sure that Grumpy had planned to move the animals secretly, so that the students wouldn't have a chance to complain any further.

"The pets will be removed later today and will be given new homes," Mr. Grundy went on, speaking even more loudly as some people began to mutter and complain to one another. "Silence, please, and let me finish! Whatever some of you may think, a school is no place to keep animals!"

Suddenly the sound of a dog barking could be

heard, and a chill came over Neil. The next second a very excited, heavily pregnant dalmatian romped joyfully through the open doors into the auditorium, barking loudly and looking very pleased with herself. Dotty, the naughtiest dog in the world!

CHAPTER EIGHT

Everyone in the room — including Neil and Mr. Hamley — was so shocked, they just stared open-mouthed at the dalmatian. Dotty stopped barking and gazed around at everyone, her eyes bright with interest.

Meanwhile, Mr. Grundy stood on the platform, looking down at the excited dog as if he was hallucinating.

"What . . . ?" he spluttered, but he was so taken aback, he couldn't finish the sentence.

Neil was just about to try to grab hold of Dotty, when Mr. Hamley finally pulled himself together and hurried forward from the back of the room. "Dotty!" he said in a trembling voice. "Come here, you bad girl!"

Dotty bounded toward him, then decided she didn't want her fun cut short just yet. Gleefully she evaded Mr. Hamley and raced toward the platform. Mr. Grundy began to back away, looking alarmed, and some of the students began to giggle. Neil couldn't help smiling, too.

"Dotty!" Mr. Hamley shouted as the dog began to paw happily at the principal's spotless pants. "Come here, *now!*"

Dotty ignored him. Getting tired of Mr. Grundy, who wasn't much fun, she jumped down off the platform and trotted to the other side of the auditorium. Mr. Hamley ran after her, skidding on the highly polished floor. Emily's teacher, Mrs. Rowntree, who was at the piano, got up and made a grab for her, but Dotty raced past, obviously having a wonderful time.

"Dotty!" Emily called out as the dalmatian got closer to where she was sitting with her class. "Come here, girl!"

Dotty hurried over eagerly. Emily grabbed her collar and hung onto it for all she was worth.

"Well done, Emily!" Mr. Hamley called, rushing toward them. "Keep her there!"

That was easier said than done. As Mr. Hamley reached them and took the dog's leash from his pocket, Dotty made another determined break for freedom. She pulled herself away from Emily and raced to the back of the room. Mr. Hamley followed her, almost tripping over the leash that had fallen to the floor. Most of the kids had stood up to see what was going on, and the teachers were trying to make them all sit down again. So was Mr. Grundy.

"Sit down!" he roared, but no one took any notice.

"This is better than TV!" Hasheem whispered to Neil.

"Yeah, except Grumpy isn't laughing!"

Suddenly Neil had an idea. He put his hand into his pocket and pulled out some of the dog treats he always carried. "Here, Dotty!" he called, shaking the packet as the dog came close to him. "Here, girl!"

Dotty stopped in her tracks as she saw the treats, and her eyes lit up. She eagerly dashed over to Neil, who gave her a couple and then grabbed her collar. Chris hurried to help him and they both hung on to Dotty until Mr. Hamley joined them, red in the face. Emily followed, holding Dotty's leash, and the whole school cheered as Mr. Hamley finally attached it to Dotty's collar.

"*Silence!*" Mr. Grundy shouted. "And *sit down!*" He strode across the floor to where Mr. Hamley was desperately clinging to his mischievous dog. He glared at Mr. Hamley, then craned forward and peered at Dotty. "I take it this *animal* is yours, Mr. Hamley?"

Mr. Hamley nodded, looking deeply embarrassed. Dotty looked up, her eyes sparkling, and leaped eagerly forward to greet this new friend. In the force of Dotty's enthusiastic hello, Mr. Grundy lost his balance and landed firmly on his bottom on the hard floor. As the whole school watched in stunned silence, Dotty planted a paw on their principal's shoulder and gave his cheek a warm, friendly lick.

Mr. Grundy looked up furiously at Mr. Hamley. "Get that disgusting creature out of *my* school!" he roared. Then he climbed to his feet, took a neatly folded handkerchief from his pocket, and wiped his face clean.

Looking shell-shocked, Mr. Hamley walked out of the auditorium with Dotty trotting obediently at his side.

"Do you think he's going to fire Mr. Hamley?" Neil whispered to Hasheem, horrified, as the principal walked determinedly to the front of the room. But before Mr. Grundy had a chance to say anything, a tall young man with a ponytail and a camera popped his head through the doorway. Emily's face lit up when she saw him, and she turned to glance at Neil a few rows behind her.

"Sorry to interrupt," the man said, "but there's no one in the office."

"And who are you?" Mr. Grundy snapped.

"Jake Fielding, *Compton News*." Jake took out his notebook. "Have you got any comment to make about your decision to get rid of the school pets?"

"I think you'd better leave," Mr. Grundy said through gritted teeth. "We're in the middle of an assembly."

"*Are* you getting rid of the school pets?" Jake asked, flipping through his notebook.

"Yes, he is," Neil said quickly. Mr. Grundy shot him an angry glance.

"And there's a petition to try and get you to change your mind, right?" Jake went on.

"Yes, there is!" Emily piped up.

"So will you give me an interview after the assembly?" Jake asked again. "To give your side of the story?"

"Certainly not!" Mr. Grundy snapped. "Who told you about that ridiculous petition?"

"Sorry, I never reveal my sources."

"Well, I can guess." Mr. Grundy's angry gaze

swept across the room and picked out Neil, Emily, and Chris. "You are three of the most undisciplined children it has ever been my misfortune to teach!"

Jake wrote that down in his notebook, and Mr. Grundy almost blew a fuse.

"Get off these premises before I call the police," he snapped. Then he eyed Neil, Emily, and Chris sternly. "Go and wait in my office, and I'll see you after assembly!"

His tone was venomous, and Neil couldn't help feeling afraid. Was the principal going to expel them, as well as fire Mr. Hamley? Things were really getting out of hand, and they hadn't even done anything wrong. Suddenly Neil felt extremely angry. *"No,"* he said quietly. "We're not going anywhere."

Mr. Grundy looked as if he was going to faint with shock, and Emily turned around again to stare at her brother in amazement. *"What* did you say, Neil Parker?"

"I said no." Neil remained exactly where he was sitting on the floor. "We haven't done anything wrong. All we wanted to do was keep our pets, and we're not moving until you reconsider!"

"Is this a demonstration?" Jake Fielding asked, focusing his camera. "Cool!"

"Neil, do you know what you're doing?" Hasheem whispered in his ear.

Neil shrugged. He was trembling with fear at the action he'd taken, but he'd had enough of Mr. Grundy trampling over everyone's feelings. This was the only thing left that he could think of.

"No pictures!" Mr. Grundy yelled at Jake. Then he turned to the rest of the students and teachers. "Assembly has been canceled," he announced. "Stand up, please."

No one moved.

"Stand up, please!" Mr. Grundy shouted, but again no one moved.

"Looks to me like the demonstration's spread to the whole school," Jake remarked. "Have you got any comment *now,* Mr. Grundy?"

"No," muttered the principal, who had turned pale. He stared helplessly at the rows of students around him, and Neil felt his heart pounding with a mixture of fear and delight. Everyone in the school was supporting them! Surely Mr. Grundy couldn't ignore the *whole school*?

"I order you all to stand *up!*" the principal roared. "This insubordination won't get you anywhere!"

"What's going on here?" asked a surprised voice, and a tall, middle-aged man in horn-rimmed glasses walked into the room. Neil glanced at Chris and Emily and raised his eyebrows. It was Mr. Bingham, the chairman of the school board! Mr. Grundy took one look at him and collapsed like a burst balloon. "Hello, Mr. Bingham," he blustered nervously. "I, er . . . wasn't expecting you this morning."

"So I see," Mr. Bingham remarked coldly.

"We're protesting about Mr. Grundy taking away our classroom pets, sir," Neil said quickly before the principal had a chance to say anything.

Mr. Bingham raised his eyebrows. "Really? Well, that's why I'm here. I got a call from the *Compton News* this morning, asking me for my reaction to this news."

"That was me," Jake put in, still writing furiously.

"So, since I didn't know anything about it," Mr. Bingham went on, "I thought I'd better come here and find out." He eyed the principal sternly. "Perhaps we ought to go and have a talk in your office, Mr. Grundy. Meanwhile —" he looked at Neil — "I think you should all go back to class while we discuss the issue of the school pets in more detail."

That was good enough for Neil. He stood up, and so did everyone else. As they all filed out, Neil felt his legs shaking so much he could hardly walk. Although it looked like he might have gotten away with it, he could have been in serious trouble for disobeying the principal.

"Brilliant move, Neil!" Hasheem slapped Neil on the back as they went into the classroom. "You really showed up old Grumpy!"

The rest of Mr. Hamley's class broke into spontaneous applause, and Neil blushed.

"I didn't do anything much," he muttered. "Anyway, we still don't know what's going to happen to Mr. Hamley."

The class fell silent.

"Looks like old Smiler might be out on his ear," Hasheem said solemnly.

Neil nodded. No doubt they would find out Mr. Hamley's fate, as well as that of the school pets, soon enough. But at the moment, all they could do was wait.

The rest of the morning was difficult. Because Mr. Hamley was out, Neil's class was split up and sent to other classrooms to work. He was on edge all the time and he couldn't concentrate. At lunchtime he met up with Chris and they went to the classroom to see if Mr. Hamley had come back. He hadn't.

While they were there, Emily came in.

"I just wanted to see what had happened to Mr. Hamley," she said anxiously.

"We don't know, but his stuff's still here." Neil pointed at the books and papers strewn over the teacher's desk. "That's a good sign."

"Do you really think Grumpy will fire him?" Emily asked.

Neil wondered how Mr. Hamley would cope if he

did get fired, what with the new baby and Dotty and her puppies to look after. "We'll have to wait and see."

They didn't have to wait much longer, though, because just then the teacher walked into the classroom with a stack of papers in his hand. "What are you three doing in here?" he asked. "You should be outside." But he didn't really look angry.

"How's Dotty, Mr. Hamley?" Neil asked. He'd never thought he'd be so happy to see Smiler again.

"All that excitement didn't tire her out, if that's what you're worried about!" Mr. Hamley said with a wry smile.

"You're not leaving, are you?" Emily asked.

Mr. Hamley shook his head, looking embarrassed. "Mr. Bingham's sorted everything out," he said quickly. "Now off you go to lunch."

"Has anything been decided about the school pets, sir?" Emily asked in a determined voice.

Mr. Hamley hesitated, then gave her one of the sheets of paper he was holding. Neil saw that it was another letter to take home to their parents.

"There has been a reconsideration concerning the decision to remove the classroom pets," Emily read. *"There have been several objections to the plan, so it has been decided that the animals will remain in school for the foreseeable future."*

"Yes!" Emily punched the air triumphantly, and

Neil and Chris grinned at each other. It had been a long struggle, but they'd finally won!

"You're staying, Tom and Jerry!" Neil said, bending over the gerbils' cage.

"I'm sure they're very pleased," said Mr. Hamley drily, beginning to look more like his old self every minute. "Now will you *please* go outside?"

"I knew we'd do it!" Emily crowed as they hurried out.

"Maybe from now on Grumpy'll take more notice of us!" Chris added.

Neil nodded, but, although he was just as pleased as the other two, he was secretly a little nervous about how Mr. Grundy would treat *him* in the future. Because, after that demonstration in the school auditorium, he was now a marked man as far as the principal was concerned.

CHAPTER NINE

"That was Mr. Carter." Bob put the phone down, looking grim. "He'll be here in twenty minutes to get Duke."

Neil, who had just walked into the office, felt himself go cold all over. "Did you tell them what happened?"

Bob shook his head.

"It's better done face-to-face. I'm going to call Sergeant Moorhead and get him here right away. Could you go and find your mother, Neil?"

Carole Parker was in the rescue center kneeling down outside Star's pen. The shaggy little dog was pressed right up against the fence, enjoying all the attention Carole was giving him. Neil smiled to himself as he stopped in the doorway to watch. Star was certainly helping his mother to rediscover her love of dogs, he thought. But she still hadn't gotten up enough courage to go inside the pen.

Carole hadn't noticed that Neil was there. She stood up and brushed herself down as Star continued to paw at the fence. Then she reached into her pocket and took out a bunch of keys.

Neil's heart began to hammer with excitement as he saw his mother unlock the door of Star's pen. She hesitated for a moment. Then she pushed the door open and went in. Star barked happily and flung himself at Carole, climbing up onto her knees as she knelt down, and licking her face. Carole took the dog in her arms and hugged it lovingly as Neil hurried toward them. He was thrilled, but he wasn't going to say so. His mom obviously wanted to pretend that nothing had been wrong.

Carole looked up and saw him as she tickled Star's tummy. "And what have you been up to, Neil Parker?" she asked, eyebrows raised.

Neil didn't know what she meant, until Carole walked over to Star's basket and picked up her sweatshirt. Then Neil remembered that he'd forgotten to take it with him when he'd sneaked into Star's pen earlier that morning. The little dog must have dragged it into his basket. "I was just trying to help," he muttered sheepishly.

Carole came out of Star's pen and gave Neil a quick hug. "Thanks," was all she said, but Neil knew that she'd guessed what he had done. They smiled at each other. He couldn't wait to tell Emily that everything would be back to normal now.

Then, with a sickening jolt, Neil remembered why he was there. "The Carters are on their way to get Duke."

Carole nodded. "Then we'd better go and wait for them."

Sergeant Moorhead had just arrived and was in the office with Bob.

"Dad, can I stay while you talk to the Carters?"

Neil asked. He really wanted to know what was going to happen to Duke.

His father hesitated, then nodded. "All right, Neil, but you must keep quiet, OK?" He looked out of the window as a red car pulled onto the driveway. "Here they are."

Neil felt nauseous as he watched Mr. and Mrs. Carter getting out of their car. He tried to imagine how *he* would feel if he and Sam were in the same situation as the Carters and Duke. He couldn't bear to think about that.

Bob went out to meet the couple and escorted them into the office. The Carters saw Sergeant Moorhead and stopped short in the doorway.

"What's going on?" Mr. Carter asked, swallowing nervously. He was a short man with glasses and gray hair.

"I'm afraid we've had some trouble with Duke —" Bob began, but that was as far as he got. To everyone's horror, Mrs. Carter immediately burst into tears.

"What sort of trouble?" Mr. Carter asked as Carole handed his wife a tissue. His gaze fell on Carole's bandaged hand, and he turned pale. "Has Duke . . . ?" But he couldn't finish the sentence.

"Duke bit my wife very badly," Bob said. "I take it this isn't the first time he's done it?"

Mr. Carter hesitated.

"It's best to be honest about these things, Mr. Carter," Sergeant Moorhead said gently.

"Duke's always been a little aggressive," Mr. Carter muttered, looking upset. "Not to us, but to people he doesn't know very well."

"What's his history?" Bob asked.

"We don't know. He's a stray we found a couple of years ago."

"And he's done this before?"

Neil waited anxiously for the Carters to reply.

Mr. Carter nodded reluctantly. "He's bitten our daughter and a neighbor. And —"

At that point Mr. Carter's wife nudged him and he stopped abruptly.

"Tell us exactly how many people Duke has bitten," Sergeant Moorhead persisted.

"Five," Mr. Carter admitted reluctantly. Well . . ." He looked at Carole. "Six."

"But he's always fine with us," Mrs. Carter said tearfully. "He's a real softie."

"You should have told us, Mr. Carter." Neil could tell his father was furious, even though he spoke calmly. "Your dog could have attacked one of my children."

The Carters looked stricken.

"S-s-sorry," Mr. Carter stammered. "We didn't think of that."

"Do you have grandchildren?" Sergeant Moorhead asked. The Carters nodded.

"And are you happy about Duke being around them?"

"Well, no . . ." Mr. Carter shuffled his feet, looking embarrassed. "Our daughter won't let the kids come over unless Duke's locked in the garden shed, because once he . . ." Then he stopped.

"You mean the dog's gone for one of your *grandchildren*?" Carole asked, horrified.

"He didn't mean it," Mr. Carter said weakly, but even he didn't look convinced.

"I'm going to be blunt, Mr. Carter," Bob said quietly. "A dog that has bitten people so many times is dangerous, especially since we don't know his history. If Duke was younger, I might have suggested some sort of behavior therapy, but as it is . . ."

Neil inhaled sharply.

Bob Parker paused, then went on very gently, "The only sensible and kind solution would be to have Duke put down."

Mrs. Carter burst into tears again, and Mr. Carter didn't look too far from an outburst of emotion, either.

"But you — you can't force us to do that?" he asked in a trembling voice.

Bob shook his head. "No one's forcing you to do anything," he assured them. "But Sergeant Moorhead has recommended that if you don't agree, the matter should be taken to court to let a judge decide. With Duke's history, it's likely that a destruction order will be granted."

"We *have* discussed this before." Mr. Carter looked anguished. "We know Duke's unpredictable. We hoped he would just calm down."

Bob shook his head. "It's gone too far for that."

Neil watched silently, wondering what the Carters would decide to do.

"He's right, you know, Daphne," Mr. Carter said miserably, taking his wife's hands. "We've been putting this off long enough. It's not fair to us *or* Duke. What if he hurt someone seriously? We'd never forgive ourselves."

Mrs. Carter nodded and wiped her eyes. "Can we see him?" she asked tremulously.

Bob nodded, and he and Sergeant Moorhead led them out of the office. Neil followed them quietly.

Duke was lying in his basket. But as soon as the Carters entered Kennel Block One, he shot to his feet, barking, and began to run around his pen. The transformation was remarkable. The large black dog had suddenly come to life again. Neil watched unhappily from the doorway as his father let the Carters in.

"Hello, boy!" Mr. Carter said in a strained voice as he knelt down to stroke Duke. Mrs. Carter flung her arms around the dog's neck.

Neil felt a lump come into his throat. It must be dreadful to know that the dog you love is going to be put to sleep. He suddenly thought of Sam and he had to blink hard to stop the tears. His mother came up quietly behind him and slid an arm around his shoulders.

"Horrible, isn't it?" she said in a low voice. "But it's for the best, Neil. Duke is too unpredictable."

"I know," Neil muttered.

"And I've got some good news that might cheer you up," Carole went on. "A Ms. Sanderson just phoned. She thinks Star might be her dog."

"That's great." But although Neil was glad that Star might be reunited with his owner, he still couldn't help feeling bad about Duke who wouldn't be going home ever again.

*   *   *

"What? I don't believe it!" Neil stared at Hasheem, his eyes wide with amazement. "Is this one of your jokes, Hasheem? Because if it is . . ."

"No joke!" Hasheem shook his head. "Mr. Grundy's resigned! It's all over the school!"

Neil had had a difficult weekend. Although his mother was now back to normal and Star (real name Dougal) had been returned to his delighted owner, the removal of Duke to Mike Turner's clinic to be put to sleep had affected everyone badly at King Street Kennels. Now Neil could hardly take in what Hasheem was telling him. Mr. Grundy was leaving? It didn't seem possible.

"How do you know, Hasheem?" he asked cautiously.

"Kathy Jones told me!"

"And how does *she* know?" Neil persisted.

"Someone else told her, I suppose!" Hasheem grinned. "Maybe he didn't want to wait for the *Compton News* to come out on Friday and make him look like a real idiot!"

"Well, I won't believe it until it's official," Neil said. Then he saw Mr. Hamley walking into the playground with Dotty trotting along beside him.

"Maybe it *is* true!" Chris nudged Neil. "I don't think Smiler would be bringing Dotty to school if Mr. Grundy was still here."

"Sir!" Neil ran over to Mr. Hamley. "Is it true that Mr. Grundy's leaving?"

Mr. Hamley looked taken aback. "Who told you that?" Then he smiled reluctantly. "It's impossible to keep anything a secret in this school! Yes, it's true. Mr. Grundy has decided to look for a position at another school."

Neil knew that Hasheem and Chris were thinking the same thing as he was. *Good riddance!*

"Under the circumstances, Mr. Bingham said it was all right for me to keep Dotty in the boiler room," Mr. Hamley went on. "So I'd be very grateful if you could help me to keep an eye on her. *Officially* this time."

"We'd love to, sir!" Neil agreed, patting Dotty's sleek head.

"I, er . . . have to meet with the board at lunchtime, so if you could spend some time with Dotty then?" Mr. Hamley barely had time to finish the sentence before Dotty lunged forward, barking at the top of her voice. Everyone turned to see Mr. Grundy, his arms full of folders and books, hurrying across the playground as if he couldn't get out of the place fast enough.

"Do you think we should say good-bye?" Hasheem asked jokingly.

"That's enough, Hasheem," Mr. Hamley said sternly. But Neil could tell that the teacher was relieved, too.

Mr. Grundy was glaring at them as he came closer, obviously planning to walk past them with his nose in the air. But Dotty had other ideas. As Mr. Grundy approached, she bounded forward to say hello.

"Get off!" Mr. Grundy roared. He leaped backward to avoid the dalmatian, then staggered and fell, dropping everything he was carrying. Neil could hardly keep a straight face as he, Hasheem, and Chris went to help the ex-principal pick up his belongings.

"I'm sorry, Mr. Grundy," Mr. Hamley apologized, but Mr. Grundy, who was fishing one of his books out of a puddle, ignored him. Red-faced with fury, he grabbed everything from the three boys without so much as a thank-you. Then he stomped across the playground, jumped into his car, and drove off.

"I think he's as glad to see the last of us as we are to see the last of him!" Chris said as Mr. Hamley took Dotty into school.

"Yeah. I wonder who'll take over now?" Hasheem remarked.

"Didn't you hear what Mr. Hamley said?" Neil pointed out. "He's got a meeting with the board today. I bet Smiler's being interviewed for the principal's job again!"

"Well, let's hope he gets it this time!" Hasheem remarked. "Or we might end up with another Grumpy Grundy!"

Although Neil was sure that Mr. Hamley's "meeting" with the board was in fact an interview, Mr. Hamley did not mention it all morning. He worked the class hard right up until lunchtime, but nobody complained. The atmosphere all around the school felt a lot happier now that Mr. Grundy was gone.

"Have you heard?" Emily yelled happily as she raced up to Neil and Chris in the corridor.

"Yes, we've heard!" Neil grinned at her. "And we think Smiler's up for the job!"

"Really?" Emily looked pleased.

Just then Hasheem ran to catch up to them. "Are you going to see Dotty now?" he asked.

Neil explained to Emily that they were keeping an eye on Dotty while Mr. Hamley was with the board, and she decided to go to the boiler room with them.

"I'm going to keep my fingers crossed that Mr. Hamley gets the job," Emily remarked as they went down the corridor to the boiler room.

"He deserves it." Neil pulled the door open. "He's had some pretty bad luck lately. Hello, Dotty! Dotty?"

Neil and the others stared into the boiler room. The dog basket was empty.

Dotty had vanished.

CHAPTER TEN

"Where *is* she?" Emily gasped. A swift search of the room had revealed nothing.

"We've got to find her!" Neil said. "She must be somewhere around the school!" They all hurried back along the corridor, keeping a sharp lookout for Dotty, and checking all the classrooms on the ground floor. There were no children in there because everyone had gone for lunch, but there were no dogs, either. They looked inside the gym, too, but it was deserted.

"Maybe she's gone to find Mr. Hamley," Hasheem suggested.

"But he's having an interview in the school office!" Chris said. "If Dotty had turned up there, Mr. Hamley would've brought her straight back."

"You don't think she might have gone outside?" Emily asked, her face pale with worry. "She might even have managed to get out of the playground!"

Neil was thinking hard. "I'm sure Dotty would have gone wherever she could pick up Mr. Hamley's scent," he said slowly, "and if she didn't go to the office —"

"She could have gone to your classroom!" Chris broke in. "Neil, you're a genius!"

They all raced for the stairs. Neil was in front, taking two steps at a time. They hurried into Mr. Hamley's room and looked around.

The classroom, which always looked bigger when there were no children in it, seemed empty. Apart from the rows of tables and chairs, there was a bigger desk near the window where Mr. Hamley sat. Then Emily clutched Neil's arm.

"Look!"

Dotty was lying underneath the teacher's table next to the wastebasket. Mr. Hamley's overcoat had been thrown over the back of his chair and the dalmatian, recognizing the scent, had dragged it off and made herself a nest on the floor. Alarmed, Neil saw that Dotty was on her side, panting, and that every so often her bulging stomach moved, as if the puppies inside were impatient to be born. He turned to the others. "Dotty's having her pups!"

"What?" Hasheem gasped. "Now?"

"Puppies don't wait for the right moment," Neil

said grimly. He checked Dotty again. He didn't think she was ready to give birth immediately, but it could be really soon. "Hasheem, go and ask the secretary to call Mike Turner, and I'll find Mr. Hamley."

"But you said he was having an interview!" Chris said.

"That's just too bad!" Neil ran out the door and down the corridor. Dotty was more important than any interview. And he knew that Mr. Hamley would feel the same way.

When Neil got to the school office, the doors were closed, but he knocked and went straight in. Mr. Hamley was sitting in front of a long table, with all the school-board members, including Mr. Bingham, grouped around it.

". . . and I have plenty of ideas to make the school a more attractive and child-friendly place if I'm appointed principal," Mr. Hamley was saying. "For instance —"

"Sorry to interrupt, sir," Neil blurted out as everyone, including Mr. Hamley, glared at him, "but Dotty's puppies are on their way!"

Mr. Hamley's face changed. "But they're early!" Then he pulled himself together quickly and jumped up. "I'm afraid I have to leave," he said to Mr. Bingham.

The chairman looked astonished. "I see. You do realize, Mr. Hamley, that this will affect your application?"

The teacher nodded. "I'm very sorry, but I must go."

"I didn't mean to interrupt," Neil apologized as they left the room.

"Don't worry." Neil was glad to hear that the teacher sounded sincere. "I couldn't let Dotty go through this alone."

There was quite a crowd in the classroom when Neil and Mr. Hamley got back, as more pupils had come inside to see what was going on. Neil was glad to see that they were all sitting quietly, so they wouldn't upset Dotty, and that Chris and Emily had moved some of the chairs and tables, and the wastebasket, to give Dotty some space. He took a quick look at the dalmatian and saw that the contractions of her abdomen were coming more quickly. It looked like she was already in the second stage of labor.

"I think she's in the second stage," Mr. Hamley said confidently, kneeling down to examine Dotty. He flushed slightly as Neil looked amazed. "I've been reading up on it," he explained, "and I helped my sister deliver her dog's puppies a few months ago."

"How long will it be before the puppies are born, sir?" asked Julie Baker, one of Emily's friends.

"Not long," Mr. Hamley said, and there was a ripple of excitement around the room. "See how Dotty's sides are heaving as the puppies move down the birth canal?"

"Did the secretary call Mike?" Neil whispered to Hasheem.

Hasheem nodded. "He's out on another house call, but he'll get here as soon as he can."

Everyone listened intently as Mr. Hamley explained how the puppies would be born. Even Neil was surprised by how knowledgeable he was. The teacher had brought some old towels to school with him, and he placed some of them around Dotty's hindquarters.

"I may need to clean up the puppies myself when they're born," he told the watching crowd. "Sometimes the mother isn't quite sure what to do. Ah, here comes the first one!"

Dotty panted hard and pushed, and a small bundle began to appear, wrapped in what looked like a transparent bag. Dotty gave an extra push and the bundle slid out onto the towel. The students who'd never seen this before, stared in amazement.

"Yuck!" Julie whispered. "What's all that stuff around the puppy?"

"That's just the sac that protects the puppy while it's growing inside the mother," Mr. Hamley explained quickly. "And see the cord? That feeds the puppy until it's born."

Neil wondered if the dalmatian was going to need help to break the sac open and release the puppy, like Delilah had when her puppies were born. But Dotty instinctively reached out and gently broke the sac with her teeth. A clear liquid poured out and for the first time they could all see the tiny, white puppy more clearly.

"But it hasn't got any spots!" Hasheem exclaimed.

Mr. Hamley smiled. "The spots will appear later as it gets older. Now we've got to make sure that we clear this little one's airways so that he can breathe." He looked at Neil. "Would you like to do the honors? You're probably more of an expert than I am!"

Thrilled, Neil carefully took the puppy from the teacher. It wriggled as he gently cleaned its face.

"Well done, Dotty!" Neil murmured. He put the puppy down close to its mother's tummy, and it floundered around for a moment before latching on to one of her teats to feed.

"How many puppies will she have, sir?" Chris asked.

"Dalmatians can have quite a few in one litter," Mr. Hamley replied. "Often seven or more."

Suddenly he stopped and glanced toward the door. The board members were standing in the doorway, watching what was going on.

"Please go on!" Mr. Bingham said with a smile. "We're enjoying the lesson as much as the children obviously are."

Mr. Hamley looked uncertain, but Neil leaped in to distract him. "I think another pup's on the way!" he said urgently.

"Right." Mr. Hamley forgot all about the board members and bent over Dotty again. "Come on, girl. You can do it!"

"Eight puppies!" Emily said ecstatically as she, Neil, and Chris walked up the Hamleys's sidewalk. "Can you believe it?"

"I don't think the school board could!" Neil laughed. "Their eyes almost popped out along with the puppies!"

Everything had gone without a hitch. Mike Turner had arrived just before the last puppy was born, and he had praised Mr. Hamley's calm handling of the situation. He had also helped the teacher to transport Dotty and her newborn offspring back home. It wasn't considered a good idea to move a new mother and her pups, but Mike had felt it was worth the risk to get Dotty back to familiar surroundings and restore order to the classroom. Mr. Hamley had been very grateful to Neil and the others and had told them to stop by for a few minutes after school if they wanted to have another quick look at the puppies.

"Ah, here you are!" beamed Mr. Hamley as he opened the door. "Come in, Dotty's expecting you!"

Neil grinned. He'd never seen Smiler looking *quite* so *smiley*!

Mrs. Hamley had just arrived back from Manchester and was sitting on the sofa with her baby on her knee. Dotty was lying in her basket in front of the fire. The dalmatian was dozing, but she opened her eyes and wagged her tail proudly as they went in. The puppies were snuggled up against their mother's warm tummy, all fast asleep.

"She's just fed them," Mrs. Hamley said proudly, "so they're *all* tired out!"

"Aren't they beautiful?" Emily knelt down and gently scratched the nearest pup's head. He snuffled a little but didn't wake up.

"I'm sorry about your interview, Mr. Hamley," Neil said, patting Dotty.

"Oh, that." Mr. Hamley didn't look very worried at all. "Well, maybe you'll find out tomorrow just who your new principal is . . ."

"You mean you got the job?" Neil grinned.

Mr. Hamley shrugged. "I didn't say that, did I?" The doorbell rang, and he went out. "Must be some more of your admirers, Dotty!"

"He *did* get the job!" Neil whispered to the others. "The board must have been impressed with the way he handled the birth of the puppies!"

"Well, *I* learned a lot for sure!" Chris agreed.

Mr. Hamley came back with Neil's parents and Sarah.

"We just had to see Dotty's pups," Carole explained as they gathered around the basket. "Everyone's talking about the dramatic way they arrived!"

Mr. Hamley smiled. "I'm just glad that Neil got me so quickly."

Neil looked down at the sleeping pups. Everything had turned out all right in the end. *Except for Duke,* he thought, his heart sinking just for a moment. Duke had once been a tiny puppy like this.

But Neil knew that life had to go on. And if the pups turned out to be anything like their mother, there was a whole lot of fun, as well as chaos, ahead!

"Well done, Dotty!" he said. "I think you're going to make a great mom!"